Whispers of the Willow:
The Chronicles of Finn and the Hidden Truth

I0614347

The
Shadow
Beneath the
Leaves

✳ ·········• Book One •········· ✳

Anthony Ofili Nwosisi

 LUCIDBOOKS

Shadow Beneath the Leaves
Book 1 of The Chronicles of Finn and the Hidden Truth

Copyright © 2025 by Anthony Ofili Nwosisi

Published by Lucid Books in Houston, TX
www.LucidBooks.com

ISBN: 978-1-63296-807-4 (Paperback)
ISBN: 978-1-63296-808-1 (Hardback)
eISBN: 978-1-63296-809-8

Special Sales: Most Lucid Books titles are available in special quantity discounts. Custom imprinting or excerpting can also be done to fit special needs. Contact Lucid Books at Info@LucidBooks.com

Disclaimer
This book is a work of fiction. Names, characters, places, and incidents are either the product of the author's imagination or used fictitiously. Any resemblance to actual persons, living or dead, events, or locales is entirely coincidental. The interpretations of any themes or events within this book are subjective and belong to the author's creative vision, meant to convey universal truths through the lens of allegory and imagination.

✶ ········ Dedication ········ ✶

To those who wander beneath ancient canopies, who walk the winding paths of life with both fear and wonder in their hearts, *Whispers of the Willow: The Chronicles of Finn and the Hidden Truth* is for you.

To the curious souls, like young Finn, who find themselves questioning the shadows that loom large and obscure the light; to those who, despite their doubts, still venture forth into the unknown, seeking truth, seeking hope—this journey is yours as much as it is Finn's. You, who are brave enough to confront the darkness within and without, to face the fears that others might ignore or deny—you are the heroes of your own story, and your courage lights the way for others.

To the wise and patient, like Willow, Griselda, Cormac, and Muriel, who have stood at the edge of the Everleaf Forest, watching over the ones who must step into the shadows—this series is a testament to your quiet strength and the guidance you offer when the path seems most uncertain. You who whisper words of wisdom, provide comfort in times of despair, and understand that true leadership lies not in force but in the gentle, steadfast presence of your love and care—your legacy lives on in the hearts of those you touch.

To those who have felt the weight of expectation, the burden of a destiny they did not choose—this series is a reminder that you are not alone. Finn's journey is the journey of every soul who has ever felt the pressure of the world on their shoulders and been called upon to be more than they believed they could be. It is a tribute to the strength that lies dormant within, waiting for the moment when it will be needed most.

To those who have faced the darkness and emerged on the other side—wiser, stronger but perhaps a little wearier—this series is for you. It is a story of resilience, of the light that flickers but never truly fades, of the power that comes from understanding that even the deepest shadows are not without end. Your journey has been hard, but it has also been beautiful, and this story is a testament to your endurance.

To the ones who have loved and given their hearts to others even when the path was uncertain—this series is for you. It is a celebration of the bonds that tie us together, the connections that give us strength when our own seems to falter. It is a reminder that love is the greatest force in the world, a light that can never be extinguished, no matter how dark the night.

To the readers who hold this book in their hands, who turn its pages with anticipation and wonder—this series is for you. It is a gift, a treasure trove of dreams and hopes, fears and triumphs. It is a journey that we take together, hand in hand, heart to heart. As you read, know that you are part of something larger, something timeless. You are part of a story that has been told since the beginning of time—a story of light and darkness, of courage and fear, of love and loss. And as you reach the end of these pages, remember that the journey never truly ends. It continues in your heart, in your life, in the choices you make every day.

To my family—Chizea, Fatimetu, Chizea Jr., Ofili Jr.—my unwavering stars, whose love and support guide me more faithfully than the North Star. Your faith in my aspirations empowers me to venture boldly into the unknown.

And finally, to the forest itself—to Everleaf, the Great Willow, and all the creatures who dwell within its ancient bounds—this series is for you. It is a love letter to the beauty and mystery of the natural world, to the wisdom that can be found in the rustling of leaves, the whisper of the wind, the quiet strength of a tree that has stood for centuries. You are the inspiration for this story, the beating heart that drives it forward. May your roots grow deep, your branches reach high, and your light never fade.

The Chronicles of Finn and the Hidden Truth is for all of you and for the light that lives within us all.

With love and gratitude,

Anthony Ofili Nwosisi

Whispers of the Willow
The Chronicles of Finn and the Hidden Truth

Whispers of the Willow: The Chronicles of Finn and the Hidden Truth unfolds across twelve books, each containing twelve stories that reflect the stages of Finn's journey. These books are not merely episodes of adventure; they are chapters in the profound journey of self-discovery, moral growth, and the realization of the importance of unity.

Books 1–4: The Awakening of Wisdom – In the first four books, Finn's journey begins with the realization of the darkness that threatens Everleaf. These books focus on the early stages of his intellectual and emotional awakening. Finn learns the value of patience from the tortoise, the difference between superficial knowledge and true wisdom from the crow, and the importance of inner peace from the silent stream. These lessons are foundational, laying the groundwork for the challenges he will face later.

Books 5–8: The Trials of Courage and Leadership – The middle section of the series delves into themes of courage, leadership, and moral integrity. Finn is tested by the riddle of the rustling leaves, which challenges his growing wisdom. He faces the whispering winds, where he must muster his courage in the face of fear. The guardian of the hidden grove teaches him about the responsibilities of leadership, while the serpent's silver tongue presents a trial of moral integrity, as Finn must discern truth from deception.

Books 9–12: The Revelation and Restoration – The final books bring Finn's journey to its climax and resolution. The dance of the fireflies symbolizes the unity that will be crucial to overcoming the darkness. The ancient owl's visions provide Finn with a broader understanding of his quest, showing him the interconnectedness of all life in Everleaf. In the veil of the vanishing mist, Finn confronts his deepest doubts and learns to see through the illusions that have clouded his mind. In final book, Finn uncovers the source of the darkness within and leads the creatures of Everleaf in restoring balance to their world.

Impactful Themes: A Deeper Exploration

Wisdom vs. Knowledge

Throughout the series, the distinction between knowledge and wisdom is a central theme. But what is wisdom? In our modern world, wisdom is often conflated with knowledge, yet these are far from the same thing. Knowledge is information—facts, data, and experiences catalogued in the mind. But wisdom is the art of understanding how to apply that knowledge in service of a greater good. Wisdom is discernment, the ability to see past the surface of things and grasp a deeper essence of life. It is the awareness that life is not just a series of events but a complex web of meaning, responsibility, and choice. Wisdom is about living well, not just knowing much.

Finn's journey is not just about acquiring information but about learning how to apply it meaningfully. The tortoise's lesson in patience, the crow's challenge of superficial knowledge, and the riddle of the rustling leaves all underscore the importance of wisdom—of understanding the deeper truths that lie beneath the surface of facts.

Courage and Resilience

Finn's trials often involve facing fear and uncertainty, teaching young readers that true courage is not the absence of fear but the strength to confront it. The night of the whispering winds and the veil of the vanishing mist both serve as powerful metaphors for the inner struggles we all face and must overcome as a key part of growth.

Unity and Leadership

A recurring theme in the series is the power of unity and the responsibilities of leadership. Finn learns that leadership is not about dominance but about guiding others with wisdom, compassion, and integrity. The guardian of the hidden grove and the dance of the fireflies illustrate how collective strength and unity are vital to overcoming challenges, emphasizing that we are stronger together than alone.

The Heart of the Story

Whispers of the Willow: The Chronicles of Finn and the Hidden Truth is more than just a children's book series; it is a profound exploration of the human condition, told through the lens of a young fox's journey in a mystical forest. The series invites readers to reflect on the nature of wisdom, the importance of courage, and the power of unity. Each story is a stepping stone in Finn's journey, and by extension, in the journey of every reader who joins him on this adventure.

This series is designed to captivate young minds while offering deep moral and philosophical lessons that resonate with readers of all ages. It is a work of art that speaks to the heart, challenges the mind, and ultimately, leaves a lasting impression on the soul.

This is the story of Finn, but it is also the story of all of us, as we navigate the complexities of life, seeking wisdom, facing our fears, and discovering the unseen truths that lie within.

Looking Ahead: The Journey Continues

As Finn's journey progresses, the lessons of Books 1–4, The Awakening of Wisdom, serve as the foundation for the greater trials he will face. In the upcoming parts of the series, The Trials of Courage and Leadership and The Revelation and Restoration, Finn will be tested in ways that challenge his newfound wisdom. He will learn the true meaning of courage, the responsibilities of leadership, and the interconnectedness of all life in Everleaf. These lessons will culminate in a final confrontation with the darkness that threatens his world—a confrontation that will require every ounce of wisdom, strength, and peace that Finn has gained.

So, as you finish this first part of Finn's journey, I invite you to reflect on the lessons of wisdom that have been woven into these chronicles. These are not just Finn's lessons; they are yours as well. Carry them with you as you continue to explore the world and know that the journey of wisdom is a lifelong endeavor, one that will guide you through every challenge you face.

And as you look forward to the volumes of Finn's journey, know that the best is yet to come. The trials ahead will be difficult, but with wisdom as your guide, you will be prepared to face them, just as Finn is.

A Guide to the Journey Ahead

Whispers of the Willow: The Chronicles of Finn and the Hidden Truth unfolds across twelve books, each containing twelve stories that reflect the stages of Finn's journey. These books are not merely episodes of adventure; they are chapters in the profound journey of self-discovery, moral growth, and the realization of the importance of unity.

Book	Book Title	Thematic Focus
1	The Shadow Beneath the Leaves	Introduces the creeping darkness in Everleaf and Finn's initial realization that something is amiss. Sets the stage for the quest and establishes the overarching conflict.
2	The Tortoise's Timeless Wisdom	Finn's first encounter with wisdom and patience. He learns that understanding cannot be rushed, and that true knowledge comes with time and reflection.
3	The Crow's Tempting Knowledge	Explores the theme of discerning true wisdom from superficial knowledge. Finn faces a trial where he must choose between the allure of easy answers and the depth of true understanding.
4	The Song of the Silent Stream	Finn learns the importance of inner peace and listening to the quiet truths of the heart. The stream teaches him that sometimes, silence speaks louder than words.
5	The Riddle of the Rustling Leaves	A mysterious and challenging riddle tests Finn's growing wisdom. He learns that not all answers are straightforward, and that some truths must be felt, not just known.
6	The Night of the Whispering Winds	Finn faces a test of courage during a tumultuous night. He learns that resilience and bravery are found not in the absence of fear but in facing it head-on.
7	The Guardian of the Hidden Grove	A protector figure helps Finn understand the responsibility that comes with wisdom and leadership. He learns that being a guardian is not about power but about care and protection.
8	The Serpent's Silver Tongue	Finn confronts deceit and learns the critical lesson of trusting his instincts over persuasive but misleading appearances. The serpent represents the dangers of eloquence without substance.
9	The Dance of the Fireflies	A lighter episode where Finn discovers the beauty of unity and collaboration. The fireflies symbolize how individual strengths can create something magical when combined.
10	The Vision of the Ancient Owl	Guided by an owl, Finn receives visions of the past and future. He begins to see the bigger picture of his quest and understands the interconnectedness of all life in Everleaf.
11	The Veil of the Vanishing Mist	Finn faces the final test of self-doubt and uncertainty. The mist represents the illusions and doubts that cloud his mind, which he must see through to find the truth.
12	The Unseen Truth	The culmination of Finn's journey. He uncovers the ultimate truth about the darkness, which lies within, and through unity, he restores the balance of Everleaf.

The Concept of Wisdom:
A Novel Perspective

Wisdom, in its essence, is not simply the accumulation of knowledge or the mastery of facts. It is the art of understanding oneself, the world around us, and the intricate dance between the two. Wisdom is the ability to see beyond the immediate and the obvious, to grasp the underlying patterns that shape our reality. It is not just about knowing what is but understanding why it is, and how to navigate it with grace and purpose.

In the context of Books 1–4, wisdom is portrayed as a journey rather than a destination. It is an unfolding process that begins with the willingness to listen to the whispers of the willow, the songs of the stream, and the quiet voice within. It requires patience, for wisdom cannot be forced or hurried. It requires discernment, for not all that glitters is gold, and not all knowledge is wise. And it requires inner peace, for only in stillness can the deeper truths be perceived.

Applying Wisdom to Real Life
A Practical Example

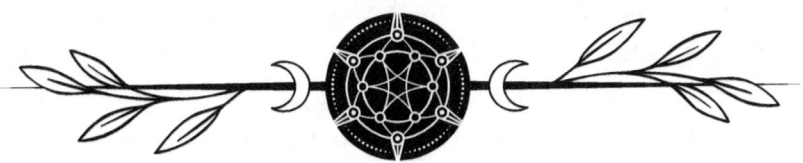

Imagine a young student, overwhelmed by the pressures of school, friends, and the expectations of society. This student feels the weight of the world on their shoulders, constantly rushing to keep up with the demands placed upon them. They seek quick solutions, often turning to shortcuts and superficial knowledge to get by. But this approach leaves them feeling empty, disconnected, and increasingly anxious.

Now, let us imagine that this student encounters the lessons of Finn's journey. They begin to understand that wisdom is not about finding the fastest route to success but about cultivating patience, discernment, and inner peace. Instead of rushing through their studies, they take the time to truly understand the material, knowing that deep learning takes time. They learn to discern what is essential and what is merely noise, focusing on what truly matters. And most importantly, they find moments of stillness in their day—whether through meditation, a walk in nature, or simply sitting quietly—allowing their minds to rest and their thoughts to settle.

As the student begins to apply these lessons, they find that their anxiety lessens, their understanding deepens, and their sense of purpose strengthens. They are no longer driven by the need to keep up with others but by a quiet confidence in their own path. This newfound peace becomes a source of strength, allowing them to face challenges with a calm mind and a steady heart.

This example illustrates how the lessons of The Awakening of Wisdom can be applied to our everyday lives. By cultivating patience, discernment, and inner peace, we can navigate the complexities of life with wisdom and grace, transforming not only ourselves but also the world around us.

THE
SHADOW
Beneath the
LEAVES

✦ ·········· Book One ·········· ✦

The Whispers Begin

I n the quiet embrace of dawn, when the first light of the
sun touches the earth with gentle fingers, the ancient
forest of Everleaf awakens. Here, beneath a canopy that
has stood for millennia, life breathes in a rhythm as old
as time itself. The air is thick with the scent of moss and
earth, and the trees, towering and majestic, stand as silent
sentinels, guardians of secrets long forgotten by the world
outside.

At the heart of this living labyrinth lies the Great Willow,
a tree unlike any other. Its roots delve deep into the soil,
drawing from the very marrow of the earth, while its
branches stretch outward like the arms of an ancient sage,
cradling the sky. The Great Willow is more than a tree; it
is the heart of Everleaf, the nexus of life and wisdom. Its

presence has shaped the lives of all who dwell within the forest, offering protection, guidance, and a sense of unity that binds every creature to the land and to each other.

In the early hours of morning, when the world is still and the dew clings to every leaf like tiny jewels, the whispers begin. These are not ordinary whispers, for they do not travel on the wind nor are they the sounds of creatures stirring from sleep. These whispers come from the very essence of the Great Willow, a low murmur that resonates through the forest, carried by the roots, the soil, and the very air. They are the whispers of knowledge, of ancient truths, passed down through the ages to those who have ears to hear and hearts to understand.

The creatures of Everleaf have always known these whispers, for they are the lifeblood of the forest. The owls, with their wide, knowing eyes, listen in reverence. The deer pause in their grazing, ears twitching to catch the murmurs. Even the playful squirrels and the shy rabbits stop in their tracks, attuned to the subtle vibrations that hum beneath their feet. It is a symphony of life, a quiet song that reassures them that all is as it should be.

But on this particular dawn, something is different. There is a subtle shift in the tone of the whispers, a faint dissonance that prickles the skin and stirs unease. The once steady, reassuring murmur of the Great Willow carries with it an undercurrent of uncertainty, a tremor that suggests something is amiss.

Prologue

It begins as a mere ripple in the fabric of the forest—a leaf that falls too soon, a shadow that lingers where there should be none. The sun, though rising, seems hesitant, its rays filtering through the branches in fragmented, hesitant beams. The birds, usually so full of song at this hour, are quiet, their voices muted as if they, too, sense the change. The very air seems heavier, laden with a weight that cannot be seen but is palpably felt.

The Great Willow, so often a symbol of strength and eternal wisdom, seems troubled. Its branches, usually so firm and resolute, shiver with a tremor that is not born of the wind. The whispers grow softer, as if the tree itself is hesitating, unsure of the message it must convey. And then, amidst the usual hum of life, there is something new—a whisper, almost imperceptible, that does not bring comfort but rather a sense of foreboding.

This new whisper is different, not just in tone but in substance. It carries with it the chill of a winter's night, the sorrow of forgotten dreams, and the fear of an unknown darkness. It is a whisper that speaks of change—of a shadow creeping through the heart of Everleaf, a shadow that is not merely the absence of light but a presence in its own right. It is a shadow born not from the outside but from within, a reflection of the doubts, fears, and uncertainties that have begun to take root in the hearts of the forest's inhabitants.

And so, as the dawn unfolds, the creatures of Everleaf find themselves on edge, their instincts telling them that something is not right. The whispers of the Great Willow,

once a source of solace, now carry a warning, a plea to be heard and heeded. There is a disturbance in the harmony of the forest, a dissonance that, if left unchecked, could unravel the very fabric of their world.

Yet, amidst this growing unease, there is a small glimmer of hope—a single, curious fox, not yet aware of the role he is destined to play, stirs from his slumber. Finn, with his sharp mind and restless spirit, will soon find himself at the center of a journey that will challenge everything he knows, a journey that will lead him deep into the heart of the darkness and beyond, to the very essence of the truth.

But for now, in this fragile moment of dawn, the forest holds its breath, poised on the brink of something profound and unknown. The whispers of the Great Willow continue, weaving through the trees, carrying with them the weight of an ancient prophecy, a call to action that will soon set the course of events in motion.

The shadow beneath the leaves is stirring, and as the day begins, so too does the journey that will determine the fate of Everleaf, the wisdom of the Great Willow, and the courage of a young fox named Finn.

This is the beginning—the whispers have changed, and nothing will ever be the same again.

Chapter 1

Finn's Curiosity

In the heart of Everleaf, where the towering trees wove their branches into a vast, verdant tapestry, there lived a fox named Finn. He was not a large fox, nor was he particularly strong. His fur was a common shade of russet, and his eyes, though sharp, did not gleam with the wisdom of age. But what set Finn apart, what made him a creature of interest among the inhabitants of the forest, was his curiosity—a curiosity as boundless as the forest itself.

From the moment he first opened his eyes to the world, Finn had been captivated by the mysteries of Everleaf. The rustle of leaves, the hum of insects, the play of light and shadow—everything was a puzzle waiting to be solved, a story waiting to be told. While other creatures were content to follow the rhythms of the forest without question, Finn's

The Shadow Beneath the Leaves

In the heart of Everleaf, where the towering trees wove their branches into a vast, verdant tapestry, there lived a fox named Finn. He was not a large fox, nor was he particularly strong. His fur was a common shade of russet, and his eyes, though sharp, did not gleam with the wisdom of age. But what set Finn apart, what made him a creature of interest among the inhabitants of the forest, was his curiosity—a curiosity as boundless as the forest itself.

From the moment he first opened his eyes to the world, Finn had been captivated by the mysteries of Everleaf. The rustle of leaves, the hum of insects, the play of light and shadow—everything was a puzzle waiting to be solved, a story waiting to be told. While other creatures were content to follow the rhythms of the forest without question, Finn's mind was always turning, always questioning, always seeking to understand the why and the how of things.

On this particular morning, as the first light of dawn crept through the canopy, Finn was already awake, his senses alert to the world around him. The air was cool and crisp, the scent of earth and dew mingling in a way that was both invigorating and calming. The Great Willow's whispers had softened with the arrival of daylight, but their presence was still felt, a subtle hum that seemed to pulse through the ground beneath Finn's paws.

He stepped out of his den, a small hollow nestled at the base of an ancient oak, and looked around. The forest was alive with the sounds of morning—birds singing their greetings to the sun, leaves rustling gently in the breeze, and somewhere in the distance, the soft murmur of a stream

winding its way through the undergrowth. It was a scene of tranquility, one that Finn had witnessed countless times before, yet it never ceased to fill him with a sense of wonder.

But today, there was something different in the air, something that tugged at the edges of Finn's awareness like a whisper he couldn't quite catch. It wasn't anything he could see or hear—no strange noise, no unfamiliar scent— just a feeling, a faint but persistent sense that the forest was not as it should be.

Finn set off on his morning exploration, his movements light and purposeful. He knew every inch of the territory surrounding his den, from the thickest brambles to the sunniest clearings. But familiarity did not dull his curiosity. Each day, he sought out new details, new changes in the landscape, new signs of life. Today was no different, except for the quiet unease that shadowed his thoughts.

As he moved through the underbrush, Finn greeted the other creatures of the forest with the ease of one who has long been part of a community. There was Willow, the wise old owl perched high in a sycamore, her golden eyes half-closed as she dozed after a night of hunting. She opened one eye as Finn passed beneath her tree, offering a slow, deliberate blink in acknowledgment.

"Morning, Finn," she hooted softly, her voice a low, soothing cadence that seemed to blend with the rustling leaves.

"Good morning, Willow," Finn replied, pausing to glance up at her. "Anything new in your neck of the woods?"

The Shadow Beneath the Leaves

Willow considered the question for a moment, her gaze drifting toward the horizon. "The winds have been restless," she said finally. "And the whispers . . . they've changed, haven't they?"

Finn nodded, a small frown creasing his brow. "Yes, they have. It's almost like they're . . . worried."

Willow's eyes narrowed slightly, but she said nothing more, merely shifting her weight on the branch before closing her eyes again. Finn took this as his cue to move on, though the owl's words lingered in his mind. The winds had been restless . . . he had felt it too, though he hadn't put it into words until now.

Farther along, Finn encountered Griselda, an elderly tortoise who had lived in Everleaf longer than most could remember. She was making her slow, deliberate way through a patch of sun-dappled ferns, her ancient shell gleaming in the morning light. Griselda was known for her wisdom, and though she seldom spoke unless she had something of importance to say, Finn always made a point to stop and chat with her.

"Morning, Griselda," Finn called out as he trotted up beside her.

Griselda paused in her journey, her dark, thoughtful eyes turning to him. "Morning, young Finn," she replied in her deep, resonant voice. "Out and about as usual, I see."

Finn grinned. "I can't help it. There's always something new to discover."

Finn's Curiosity

The tortoise gave a slow nod, her gaze drifting up toward the canopy. "Indeed. But not all discoveries bring comfort. Sometimes, they bring change."

The words, simple as they were, struck a chord in Finn. He opened his mouth to ask her what she meant, but before he could, a sudden chill ran through him—a cold, prickling sensation that started at the base of his spine and worked its way up to the nape of his neck. It was as if a shadow had passed over him, though the sun was shining bright and clear above.

Finn's ears flicked back, his eyes narrowing as he looked around. There was nothing out of place that he could see— no dark clouds, no lurking predator, nothing to explain the sudden drop in temperature. And yet, the feeling persisted, a cold knot of unease that settled in his chest.

"Did you feel that?" Finn asked, his voice a little more strained than he intended.

Griselda didn't answer right away. She tilted her head slightly, her expression unreadable. "The forest is full of whispers, Finn," she said at last. "Some are louder than others. The trick is knowing which ones to listen to."

Finn wasn't sure what to make of that, but he nodded all the same. "I'll keep that in mind," he said, though his thoughts were already elsewhere, trying to make sense of the strange sensation.

As he continued his exploration, Finn's mind was a whirl of thoughts. The whispers, the restless winds, the chill in the

air—it was all connected somehow, he was sure of it. But how? And more importantly, why? Finn had always trusted his instincts, and they were telling him now that something was very wrong.

It wasn't long before Finn's path led him to a familiar clearing, a place where the sunlight always seemed to fall just right, casting a warm, golden glow over the soft grass and wildflowers. It was one of his favorite spots in the forest, a place where he often came to think or simply enjoy the beauty of the world around him.

But today, as he stepped into the clearing, Finn froze. The light was wrong—paler, weaker than it should be. And there, in the center of the clearing where the grass should have been lush and green, was a patch of shadow. It wasn't a natural shadow, cast by the trees or a passing cloud. It was a thing unto itself—dark, cold, and utterly out of place.

Finn's heart pounded in his chest as he approached the shadow, his senses on high alert. The closer he got, the more the air around him seemed to chill, until it felt as though he had stepped into the depths of winter. He hesitated at the edge of the shadow, staring down at it with wide eyes.

The shadow didn't move, didn't change. It was simply there, a blot on the landscape, a mark of something that didn't belong. Finn reached out a tentative paw, hovering it over the darkness without touching it, as if expecting it to react in some way.

But the shadow remained still, indifferent to his presence. Finn pulled his paw back, unease coiling tighter in his gut.

Finn's Curiosity

Whatever this was, it was not something natural. He had never encountered anything like it in all his explorations, and the wrongness of it set every nerve on edge.

For a long moment, Finn stood there, wrestling with his instincts. Every fiber of his being screamed at him to run, to get away from this thing that didn't belong. But his curiosity, that relentless drive to understand, held him in place. He had to know what this shadow was, what it meant, and why it had appeared in his forest.

Finally, with a deep breath, Finn turned away from the clearing, his mind racing. There was only one place he could go for answers, one being who might know what this shadow was and what it portended. The Great Willow's whispers had guided him before, and now, more than ever, he needed its wisdom.

As Finn made his way back through the forest, the chill of the shadow still clinging to him, he couldn't shake the feeling that this was only the beginning. Something was coming, something that would change everything he knew about Everleaf and the life he had always taken for granted. And whatever it was, it had already begun to cast its shadow over the forest.

But Finn was no ordinary fox. He was a creature of curiosity, of intelligence, and of courage—courage he would need in the days to come, as the whispers of the Great Willow turned from warnings to prophecies, and the shadow beneath the leaves grew darker still.

Chapter 2

A Stranger in the Shadows

The forest was no longer the familiar sanctuary it had once been for Finn. The chill from the shadow he had encountered in the clearing still clung to him, gnawing at the edges of his thoughts, even as the warmth of the day began to permeate the underbrush. The whispering of the Great Willow, usually so comforting, now seemed tinged with an undercurrent of urgency that he couldn't quite shake.

Finn's mind raced as he moved cautiously through the forest, his senses heightened, attuned to every rustle, every flicker of movement in the periphery of his vision. The light filtering through the canopy seemed dimmer, less certain, as if the sun itself was reluctant to fully penetrate the shadows that clung to the forest floor.

The Shadow Beneath the Leaves

As he rounded a bend in the path, Finn came upon a trail he had not noticed before. It was faint, almost imperceptible, a series of indentations in the soft earth that led off into a denser part of the forest where the trees grew closer together, their branches interwoven like the fingers of giants. Finn paused, his sharp eyes tracing the path of the tracks. They were unlike any he had seen before—long, narrow, and deep, as if whatever had made them was heavier than any creature, he knew of in Everleaf.

A sense of unease settled over him, but it was accompanied by that familiar spark of curiosity, the urge to understand and explore the unknown. Finn hesitated for only a moment before he began to follow the tracks, moving silently, his paws barely making a sound on the damp earth. The air grew colder the deeper he went as the sunlight increasingly filtered through the thickening canopy, casting everything in shades of gray and green.

The path twisted and turned, leading him through a part of the forest he rarely ventured into. The trees here were ancient, their bark rough and gnarled, their roots sprawling like the veins of some great, slumbering beast. The silence was profound, broken only by the occasional rustle of leaves high above or the distant call of a bird. Yet even those sounds seemed muted, as if the forest itself was holding its breath, waiting for something.

It wasn't long before Finn noticed another sign that he was not alone. A low-hanging branch, its leaves brushed aside, revealed scratches in the bark—deep, jagged marks that spoke of claws far larger than his own. The realization sent a shiver down his spine, but instead of turning back, Finn pressed on, driven by a need to understand what he was dealing with.

As he continued to follow the trail, Finn began to notice other signs—broken twigs, trampled undergrowth, a sense that something large had passed this way not long ago. The tracks led him to a small, secluded glade, surrounded by towering oaks that seemed to form a natural barrier around it. Here, the air was even colder, the shadows thicker, and the light weaker, as if the very essence of the place was being drained away.

In the center of the glade, where the grass should have been soft and green, there was instead a patch of bare earth— ground that was scarred and torn as if something had been dragged across it. Finn crouched low, his eyes scanning the area for any sign of movement, but all was still. The silence was oppressive, pressing down on him from all sides, making it hard to think, to breathe.

Then, out of the corner of his eye, Finn saw it—a flicker of movement, a shape that seemed to materialize out of the shadows at the edge of the glade. It was a figure, indistinct and shrouded in darkness, its form shifting and elusive, as if it were part of the shadows themselves. Finn's heart raced as he strained to make out any details, but the figure remained obscure, its presence more felt than seen.

The air grew colder still, and Finn's breath came in shallow, misty puffs as he watched the figure. It moved slowly, deliberately, circling the edge of the glade, its movements

fluid and unsettling. There was something predatory about the way it moved, a quiet menace that set every nerve in Finn's body on edge.

For a moment, the figure seemed to pause, its attention turning directly toward Finn. Though he could not see its eyes, he felt its gaze on him, sharp and piercing, as if it were looking straight through him, seeing not just his form but his thoughts, his fears. Finn's instincts screamed at him to run, to flee back to the safety of the Great Willow, but he stood his ground, his legs trembling beneath him.

The figure moved again, this time closer, its outline becoming slightly clearer as it approached the center of the glade. Finn could see that it was tall, much taller than any creature he had ever encountered in the forest, its limbs long and thin, its body draped in what looked like tattered, dark fabric that billowed like smoke in the cold air. It exuded an aura of coldness, of malevolence, which seemed to seep into the ground beneath it, causing the earth to wither and die in its wake.

Finn's breath caught in his throat as the figure stopped, standing motionless in the center of the glade. For a long, tense moment, neither of them moved, as if the forest itself had frozen in time, waiting for something to happen.

Then, without warning, the figure melted back into the shadows, its form dissipating like mist in the morning sun. The chill in the air lifted slightly, the oppressive silence easing as the sounds of the forest slowly returned. But the sense of unease remained, as did the knowledge that

whatever that figure had been, it was not gone. It was still out there, lurking in the shadows, waiting.

Finn remained where he was for a long moment, his mind racing to make sense of what he had just seen. The figure, the coldness, the sense of malevolence—it was unlike anything he had ever encountered in Everleaf. It wasn't just a creature of the forest; it was something else, something darker, something that didn't belong.

Finn's thoughts turned to the other creatures of the forest— the birds, the deer, the other foxes—who had all seemed more unsettled in recent days. Had they seen this figure too? Had they felt its presence? And if they had, why hadn't they said anything? What were they so afraid of?

Questions swirled in Finn's mind as he slowly made his way out of the glade, retracing his steps along the path. He moved more quickly now, his curiosity tempered by a growing sense of responsibility. Whatever this figure was, whatever it wanted, it was a threat to Everleaf, to everything he knew and loved. And if the other creatures were too afraid to face it, then it fell to him to do something about it.

As he emerged from the denser part of the forest, the light grew brighter, the air warmer, but the chill of the encounter stayed with him, a cold knot of fear and determination lodged deep in his chest. Finn knew that he couldn't keep this to himself. He had to warn the others, had to find out what this figure was and why it was here.

The Shadow Beneath the Leaves

The Great Willow's whispers echoed in his mind, no longer just a hum in the background but a voice urging him to act, to seek the truth before it was too late. The shadow beneath the leaves was not just a phenomenon; it was an intent, a presence that sought to spread its darkness throughout the forest.

Finn's curiosity had led him to this discovery, but now it was his responsibility to protect Everleaf from the danger that lurked within its heart. He could no longer afford to be just an observer. The time had come for action, for courage, for understanding.

And so, with the figure's cold gaze still lingering in his thoughts, Finn set off once more, this time with a new resolve. He would find out what this shadow was, where it had come from, and what it wanted. And he would do whatever it took to protect his home from the darkness that now threatened to consume it.

Chapter 5

The First Signs of Darkness

The sun was rising higher in the sky as Finn made his way back through the forest, but the warmth of its rays did little to dispel the cold knot of unease lodged deep in his chest. The encounter in the glade lingered in his mind like a shadow that refused to fade, its dark tendrils weaving through his thoughts, leaving him with a sense of foreboding he couldn't shake.

Finn had always known the forest to be a place of life and vibrancy, where every leaf, every blade of grass, every creature seemed to pulse with energy and purpose. Everleaf was a sanctuary, a haven where the Great Willow's whispers guided and protected all who lived within its boundaries. But now, as Finn moved through the familiar paths, he couldn't help but notice the subtle, unsettling changes that had begun to take hold.

The Shadow Beneath the Leaves

The first sign was the silence. It was not the comforting quiet of dawn or the peaceful stillness of a midday rest, but an unnatural hush that seemed to smother the very air. The birds, usually so full of song and chatter, were silent. Not a single trill or chirp broke the stillness, and even the rustle of leaves seemed subdued, as if the trees themselves were holding their breath.

Finn paused, his ears twitching, straining to catch any sound that might break the oppressive silence. But there was nothing—no birds, no insects, no distant calls of other animals. It was as if the forest had been wrapped in a blanket of stillness, muffling all signs of life.

As he continued on, Finn noticed something else—a faint but unmistakable scent of decay. It was a smell he had only encountered in the deepest parts of the forest, where the cycle of life and death played out in the shadows, far from the vibrant heart of Everleaf. But here, in the open, it was out of place, a sharp contrast to the fresh, living scent of the trees and plants.

Finn followed the scent, his nose leading him to a small clearing he had often visited, a place where wildflowers bloomed in a riot of color, and the grass was always soft and green. But when he stepped into the clearing, his heart sank. The flowers were withered, their petals brown and shriveled, hanging limply from their stems. The grass, once lush and inviting, was dry and brittle underfoot, the green replaced by a sickly yellow.

The First Signs of Darkness

Finn's breath caught in his throat as he took in the scene. It was as if the life had been sucked out of the clearing, leaving behind only the shell of what had once been. The vibrant, living energy that had always filled this place was gone, replaced by a sense of emptiness that gnawed at the edges of Finn's mind.

He crouched low, examining the withered plants with a growing sense of dread. This was no ordinary blight or seasonal change. It was something deeper, something that struck at the very heart of the forest. The cold knot of fear in his chest tightened, and for the first time, Finn felt truly afraid—not just for himself but for Everleaf.

The silence and decay were not confined to the clearing. As Finn moved on, he began to notice other signs—subtle at first but growing more pronounced as he ventured deeper into the forest. The leaves on the trees were losing their luster, their edges curling and browning as if they had aged overnight. The air, usually filled with the hum of insects and the soft rustle of small creatures in the underbrush, was heavy and still.

Finn's mind raced, trying to piece together what was happening. The shadow he had encountered in the glade and the figure that had dissolved into the darkness—both were connected to this; he was sure of it. But how? And why was the forest reacting this way? What was the source of this creeping decay, this silence that stifled all life?

As he pressed on, Finn encountered more evidence of the forest's decline. A stream he often visited, which was usually

clear and sparkling, now ran slow and murky, its waters tinged with an unnatural brown. The fish that usually darted through the shallows were nowhere to be seen, and the plants along the bank were limp and colorless, their leaves drooping as if they had given up the fight for life.

The path led Finn to a grove of ancient oaks, their thick trunks rising like pillars into the sky. He had always found comfort in this place, surrounded by trees that had stood for centuries, their roots intertwined with the history of the forest. But now, as he stepped into the grove, Finn felt a chill run down his spine. The trees were silent, their branches bare of leaves, their bark cracked and dry.

Finn moved closer to one of the oaks, his eyes tracing the deep grooves in the bark. It was as if the tree had been drained of its life force; its once-strong presence had been reduced to a hollow shell. He placed a paw on the trunk, feeling the rough texture under his pads, but there was no warmth, no pulse of life.

The sense of dread that had been building in Finn's chest threatened to overwhelm him. This was not just a natural change or the result of a passing illness. It was something more insidious, something that was spreading through the forest like a poison, leeching the life from everything it touched.

And yet, despite the growing evidence of the forest's decline, the source of the darkness remained elusive. There was no sign of the shadowy figure he had encountered, no trace of its presence beyond the destruction it left in its wake. It was as if the shadow had no form, no substance, existing only

in the spaces between light and darkness, feeding on the fear and uncertainty it created.

Finn's thoughts turned to the other creatures of the forest. Had they noticed the changes? Had they felt the same unease, the same sense that something was wrong? He recalled the silence of the birds, the absence of other animals, the way the trees seemed to shrink away from him as he passed. It was as if the entire forest was retreating into itself, withdrawing from the light and warmth that had always sustained it.

As he walked on, Finn's concern grew. He had always known Everleaf to be a place of harmony, where every creature and plant played its part in the delicate balance of life. But now, that balance was being disrupted, and the consequences were all too clear. The forest was dying, and if the source of the darkness wasn't found and stopped, it wouldn't be long before Everleaf became a wasteland, devoid of the life and beauty it had always known.

Finn's mind raced with questions, but there were no answers to be found, only more signs of the creeping decay that was spreading through the forest. The birds were gone, plants were withering, and streams were drying up. Even the Great Willow's whispers, once so strong and reassuring, were fading, their voice growing weaker with each passing day.

Finn knew he had to do something, but what? The shadow, the figure, the decay—it was all connected, but how could he, a single fox, hope to understand, let alone stop, something so vast, so insidious? The task seemed

impossible, the weight of it pressing down on him like a physical force.

But as he stood in the middle of the dying grove, surrounded by the evidence of the forest's decline, Finn felt a spark of determination ignite within him. He couldn't allow fear to paralyze him, couldn't let the darkness spread unchecked. The forest was his home, and the Great Willow had whispered to him, guiding him, trusting him to find a way.

Finn took a deep breath, his resolve hardening. He would not let the darkness take Everleaf without a fight. He would seek out the source of the decay, uncover the truth behind the shadow, and find a way to stop it, no matter the cost.

With a renewed sense of purpose, Finn turned and began to make his way back through the forest, his eyes sharp, his ears attuned to every sound. The path ahead was uncertain, the dangers unknown, but Finn knew one thing for sure: He would not rest until he had uncovered the truth and saved his home from the darkness that now threatened to consume it.

As the sun began its slow descent toward the horizon, casting long shadows across the forest floor, Finn pressed on, the weight of his task heavy on his shoulders, but his spirit was unyielding. The first signs of darkness had appeared, but so too had the first stirrings of hope, of determination, of courage.

The First Signs of Darkness

And so, with the whispers of the Great Willow still echoing in his mind, Finn ventured deeper into the forest, ready to face whatever lay ahead, ready to protect Everleaf from the shadow that sought to destroy it. The battle for the heart of the forest had begun, and Finn was determined to see it through to the end.

Chapter 4

The Gathering of the Elders

The sky was a deepening hue of indigo as dusk settled over Everleaf, painting the forest in shades of twilight. The last remnants of sunlight filtered through the canopy, casting long, wavering shadows across the forest floor. The trees stood silent and still, their branches heavy with the weight of the coming night. The air was thick with anticipation and a sense of foreboding that had grown stronger with each passing hour.

Finn moved with purpose through the darkening woods, his heart pounding with a mixture of urgency and unease. The decay he had witnessed, the silence that smothered the forest like a heavy fog, the shadowy figure that lingered at the edges of his thoughts—all of it pointed to something far more sinister than he had initially realized. The time had come to seek answers, to consult with those who

might know more about the darkness that was spreading through Everleaf.

He knew where he needed to go—the Great Willow, the ancient heart of the forest, where the elder creatures gathered to share their wisdom and commune with the tree's whispers. It was a place of great power and even greater mystery, a sanctuary where the secrets of the forest were guarded and where the future could sometimes be glimpsed in the patterns of the leaves and the murmurs of the wind.

As he approached the clearing where the Great Willow stood, Finn felt a shiver of awe and reverence pass through him. The tree loomed before him, its massive trunk gnarled and twisted with age, its roots spreading out like the fingers of a giant, intertwining with the earth itself. The branches stretched high into the sky, cradling the stars in their embrace, while the leaves rustled softly as if whispering secrets only the wind could hear.

The clearing was already filled with the forest's elder creatures, gathered in a loose circle around the base of the Great Willow. There was Willow the owl, perched on a low-hanging branch that swayed gently in the breeze, her golden eyes glowing faintly in the dim light. Beside her stood Griselda the tortoise, her ancient shell gleaming in the fading light, her expression as inscrutable as ever. A few paces away, Cormac the stag stood tall and regal, his antlers silhouetted against the sky, while Muriel the hare huddled close to the ground, her ears twitching nervously.

The Gathering of the Elders

These were the oldest and wisest of the forest's inhabitants, the keepers of its history and the guardians of its future. They had seen many seasons come and go, had weathered countless storms and challenges, and yet, as Finn looked around at their solemn faces, he could see the same fear and uncertainty that gnawed at his own heart reflected in their eyes.

As Finn entered the circle, all eyes turned to him, and for a moment, he felt the weight of their gazes as their expectations pressed down on him like a physical force. But then the Great Willow stirred, its leaves rustling with a sound like a sigh, and the tension in the air seemed to ease slightly, as if the tree itself had acknowledged his presence and granted him permission to join the gathering. Willow the owl was the first to speak, her voice low and measured, carrying the wisdom of countless nights spent watching over the forest.

"We have all felt it . . .," she said, her words soft but firm, "the change in the wind, the silence in the trees, the darkness that creeps through our home. Everleaf is not as it was, and the Great Willow's whispers have turned to warnings."

A murmur of agreement rippled through the gathering, the other elders nodding their heads solemnly.

Griselda, her voice deep and resonant, added, "The signs are everywhere. . . plants withering where they should be thriving, streams drying up where they should flowing. . ., shadows where there should be light. This is no ordinary

change of season, no natural cycle of life and death. This is something new, something dark."

Finn listened intently, his heart beating faster as the elders spoke. They had all noticed the same things he had, felt the same sense of unease—of wrongness. But what could it mean? And more importantly, what could be done about it?

Cormac the stag, his voice strong and steady, spoke next. "We have seen many threats to our home over the years—storms, droughts, predators—but never have we faced something like this. This darkness . . . it feels . . . unnatural, as if it has a will of its own, a purpose. And yet, it remains elusive, slipping through our grasp like smoke."

At this, Muriel the hare, her voice trembling slightly, whispered, "I have felt it too . . . that presence in the shadows. It watches us, waits for us. It's as if it knows we are afraid, and it feeds on that fear."

The circle fell silent as the weight of Muriel's words hung in the air. Finn felt a chill run down his spine, the memory of the shadowy figure in the glade flashing through his mind. It had felt exactly as Muriel described—a presence, not just an absence of light but something with intent, something that had seen him, that had known him.

Before Finn could speak, the Great Willow's leaves rustled again, this time with more urgency. The sound was different now, sharper, like a warning carried on the wind. The elders fell silent, their attention turning to the tree, their expressions grave. It was Griselda who spoke next, her voice heavy with the weight of what she was about to say.

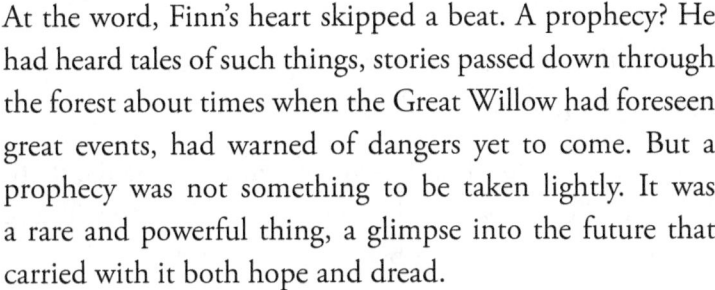

The Gathering of the Elders

"The Great Willow has been whispering to us for generations, guiding us and protecting us. But now, its whispers have turned to something more. They have become . . . a prophecy."

At the word, Finn's heart skipped a beat. A prophecy? He had heard tales of such things, stories passed down through the forest about times when the Great Willow had foreseen great events, had warned of dangers yet to come. But a prophecy was not something to be taken lightly. It was a rare and powerful thing, a glimpse into the future that carried with it both hope and dread.

"The prophecy speaks of a great darkness," Griselda continued, her voice low and solemn. "It speaks of a shadow that will spread through Everleaf, consuming all in its path. It is a darkness born not of nature but of something else, something deeper, something that has been lurking in the shadows, waiting for its time."

The other elders nodded, their faces pale in the twilight. Finn could feel tension in the air, a sense of impending doom that seemed to seep into his very bones. But there was something else in the prophecy, something more than just a warning of the darkness to come.

"And yet," Griselda said, her voice softening slightly, "the prophecy also speaks of hope. It speaks of a young fox, one who is curious and clever, one who will rise to face the darkness and bring light back to the forest."

Finn's breath caught in his throat as the elders turned to look at him, their eyes filled with a mix of expectation

and uncertainty. A young fox? Could they mean him? But how could that be? He was just Finn, a curious fox with a penchant for exploring the forest, nothing more. How could he possibly be the one the prophecy spoke of, the one who was meant to face this darkness and save Everleaf?

Willow the owl fixed him with her piercing gaze, her golden eyes seeming to see straight into his soul.

"The Great Willow has chosen you, Finn," she said quietly. "You are the one who will face the darkness, who will seek out its source and stop it before it consumes us all."

Finn felt a wave of disbelief wash over him: How could he be the one to stop the darkness? It seemed impossible, ridiculous even. He was no hero, no warrior. He was just a fox, one who loved the forest and the life within it, but who had never faced anything like this before.

"But . . . I don't understand," Finn stammered, his voice trembling with uncertainty. "How can I be the one? What am I supposed to do?"

"The prophecy does not give us all the answers," Cormac said gently, his voice filled with quiet strength. "But it tells us this much: You are the key, Finn. You have the curiosity, the courage, and the heart to seek out the truth and face the darkness head-on. The Great Willow will guide you, as it has guided all of us."

Finn looked around at the gathered elders; their faces were a mixture of hope and concern. They believed in the prophecy, believed in the Great Willow's wisdom, and now they were

placing that belief in him. The weight of it was almost overwhelming, a burden he had never expected to carry.

But as he stood there beneath the towering branches of the Great Willow, Finn felt a small flicker of resolve ignite within him. The forest was his home, the place he had explored and loved his entire life. He couldn't stand by and let it fall to darkness, not if there was something he could do to stop it.

He took a deep breath, steadying himself. "I'll do it," he said finally, his voice firmer now, though still tinged with uncertainty. "I'll find out what's causing this darkness, and I'll stop it, whatever it takes."

The elders nodded in approval, their gazes softening with pride. Willow dipped her head in acknowledgment, while Griselda gave a slow, deliberate nod. Cormac's lips curved into a faint smile, and even Muriel seemed to relax slightly, her ears drooping in relief.

"The Great Willow will be with you, Finn," Griselda said, her voice filled with quiet conviction. "You will not be alone on this journey. The forest will guide you, and we will support you in whatever way we can."

Finn nodded, his heart pounding with a mixture of fear and determination. He didn't know what lay ahead, didn't know what challenges or dangers he would face. But he knew one thing for certain: He couldn't turn back now. The prophecy had chosen him, and he would do whatever it took to fulfill it.

The Shadow Beneath the Leaves

As the gathering began to disperse, the elders moving off into the shadows, Finn remained where he was, staring up at the Great Willow. The tree's leaves rustled softly in the breeze, their whispers filled with a sense of both urgency and encouragement. Finn closed his eyes, letting the sound wash over him, drawing strength from the ancient wisdom that seemed to flow through the very air around him.

When he opened his eyes again, the sky was dark, and the first stars were twinkling faintly above. The clearing was empty now, the elders gone, but the sense of purpose that had taken root in Finn's heart remained. The forest was depending on him, and he would not let it down.

With one last look at the Great Willow, Finn turned and made his way back into the forest, his steps steady and determined. The path ahead was uncertain, but he knew now that he was not alone. The whispers of the Great Willow would guide him, and the strength of the forest would be with him.

The battle against the darkness had begun, and Finn was ready to face whatever lay ahead. The prophecy had spoken, and now, it was time for him to fulfill it.

Finn's Realization

The forest lay shrouded in darkness, the night sky a canvas of deep indigo punctuated by the soft glow of distant stars. The air was thick with the weight of the evening's revelations, and the once familiar paths of Everleaf seemed fraught with uncertainty. Finn walked slowly, his mind a whirl of thoughts, his heart heavy with the burden of the prophecy that had been laid upon him. The elders had placed their trust in him; the Great Willow had spoken of him, and yet, as he made his way back to his den, doubt gnawed at the edges of his resolve.

The quiet of the forest was profound, almost oppressive, as if the very trees were holding their breath, waiting for something to happen. Finn's paws moved silently over the earth, but his thoughts were anything but still. The

prophecy had named him, a young fox, as the one who would confront the darkness spreading through Everleaf. It had spoken of his curiosity, his courage, his heart, but as Finn replayed the words in his mind, he couldn't shake the feeling that this must be a mistake.

He was no hero, no great warrior destined to save the forest. He was just Finn—a fox who loved to explore, who found joy in the simple wonders of the world around him. How could he, of all creatures, be the one to stand against a force so dark, so insidious that even the oldest and wisest of Everleaf were at a loss to understand it? The weight of the prophecy felt too heavy, almost impossible, as if it were a mantle far too large for him to bear.

As he walked, the doubt in Finn's heart grew stronger, casting a shadow over the flicker of resolve that had sparked within him at the gathering of the elders. What if he wasn't strong enough? What if he failed? The thought of letting down the forest, of letting down the Great Willow, filled him with a deep, gnawing fear. The very idea of facing the darkness alone seemed overwhelming, like staring into a void that threatened to swallow him whole.

Lost in his thoughts, Finn barely noticed that he had wandered off the path, his paws carrying him deeper into the forest, toward the place where the Great Willow stood in solitary majesty. It was as if some part of him, beyond his conscious mind, had known where he needed to go, had sought out the ancient tree's wisdom without him even realizing it.

Finn's Realization

The Great Willow loomed before him, its massive trunk dark against the night sky, its branches stretching out like arms welcoming him into its embrace. The leaves rustled softly in the breeze, their whispers gentle and reassuring, a stark contrast to the storm of doubt raging within Finn's heart. He paused at the edge of the clearing, his eyes tracing the familiar contours of the tree, the way its roots seemed to sink into the earth as if anchoring the very soul of the forest.

For a long moment, Finn simply stood there, staring up at the Great Willow, his thoughts churning, his heart heavy. He had come to this tree countless times before seeking comfort and guidance, but never had he felt so small, so inadequate in the face of what was being asked of him. The whispers of the Great Willow had always been a source of strength for him, but now, they seemed distant and elusive as if they were speaking a language he could no longer understand.

Slowly, almost hesitantly, Finn moved closer to the tree, his steps careful and measured, as if afraid that one wrong move might break the fragile connection he sought. He reached out a paw, resting it gently against the rough bark of the Great Willow's trunk. The texture was familiar, grounding him in the reality of the moment, but it did little to ease the turmoil within him.

The whispers of the Great Willow swirled around him, a soft, persistent hum that seemed to resonate with the very air. Finn closed his eyes, focusing on the sound, trying to find meaning in the patterns of the whispers, trying to understand what the tree was telling him. He felt the

vibrations under his paw, felt the life that pulsed through the Great Willow, which was as old and enduring as the forest itself.

But the doubt remained, a heavy, dark presence that refused to be banished. What if he wasn't the one? What if the prophecy had been wrong? The thought of failing, of letting down the forest and all who depended on him, filled him with a deep, paralyzing fear. He had always believed in the strength of the Great Willow and the wisdom of the elders, but now, standing here alone in the dark, that belief wavered.

The whispers grew louder, more insistent as if the Great Willow were trying to reach him, trying to break through the wall of doubt that had risen in his mind. Finn's breath caught in his throat as the whispers seemed to form words, not in any language he knew but in a language that resonated deep within him, in the very core of his being.

"Do not fear, young one," the whispers seemed to say. "You are not alone. The strength of the forest is with you; the wisdom of the ages flows through you. The path is difficult, the burden heavy, but you are not without guidance. The Great Willow sees you, knows you, believes in you."

Finn's eyes snapped open, his heart pounding in his chest. The whispers were clear now, cutting through the fog of doubt like a beam of light piercing the darkness. The Great Willow believed in him and trusted him to carry out the prophecy, to face the darkness and restore balance to the forest. The realization hit him with the force of a wave

crashing over him and filling him with a sense of purpose he hadn't felt before.

But along with that purpose came the weight of responsibility heavier than anything he had ever known. The whispers had comforted him, yes, but they had also confirmed what he had feared—the prophecy was real, and it was his to fulfill. There was no turning back, no denying the truth of what was being asked of him.

Finn felt waves of emotion wash over him—fear, doubt, determination, all mingling together in a chaotic storm that threatened to overwhelm him. He had never wanted this, never asked to be the one chosen by the Great Willow, by the forest to carry such a heavy burden. He was just a fox, just Finn, not a hero, not a savior.

And yet, as he stood there, his paw pressed against the trunk of the Great Willow, he felt something shift within him. The doubt . . . the fear was still there, but beneath it, something else stirred—something stronger, something that had been quietly growing within him even as he had tried to deny it.

It was a sense of resolve, a deep, abiding determination that had been kindled by the whispers of the Great Willow, by the belief that the tree and the forest had placed in him. Finn had always been curious, always eager to explore and understand the world around him, but now, that curiosity was being tempered by something more—by a sense of responsibility, by the knowledge that the fate of Everleaf rested, in part, on his shoulders.

The Shadow Beneath the Leaves

Finn took a deep breath, letting it out slowly as he steadied himself. He didn't have all the answers, didn't know exactly what lay ahead or how he would face the challenges that awaited him. But he knew one thing with absolute certainty: He couldn't stand by and do nothing. The darkness was spreading; the forest was dying, and if he didn't act . . . if he didn't at least try to fulfill the prophecy, then everything he loved—everything he had ever known—would be lost.

With that thought, Finn felt the last remnants of doubt begin to melt away, replaced by a quiet, steely determination. The path ahead was uncertain, the dangers unknown, but he would face them. He would seek out the source of the darkness, uncover the truth, and do whatever it took to stop it.

The whispers of the Great Willow swirled around him, filling the air with their gentle, reassuring hum. Finn closed his eyes once more, letting the sound wash over him, letting it fill him with the strength and resolve he would need for the journey ahead.

When he opened his eyes again, the night was still, and the stars twinkled faintly above, casting a soft glow over the clearing. Finn took one last look at the Great Willow, the ancient tree that had seen so much and guided so many before him.

The whispers were quiet now, a soft murmur that seemed to say, "Go forth, young one. The forest is with you."

With a deep breath, Finn turned and began to make his way back through the forest, his steps steady and sure. The

doubt that had plagued him was still there, but it was no longer a weight around his neck, no longer a chain holding him back. The prophecy was a challenge, one that he was ready to face.

The realization had come; the truth had been accepted, and now, it was time to act. Finn was the one mentioned in the prophecy, the one chosen to confront the darkness and restore balance to Everleaf. And though the path ahead was fraught with danger and uncertainty, Finn knew that he was not alone. The Great Willow's whispers would guide him; the strength of the forest would sustain him, and the determination that had been kindled within him would carry him forward.

As he walked, the first light of dawn began to pierce the darkness, casting the forest in a soft, golden glow. Finn lifted his head, his eyes bright with the light of a new day— the light of a new purpose. The battle had not yet begun, but Finn was ready. He would face the darkness; he would seek out the truth, and he would protect the forest he loved with everything he had.

The prophecy had spoken, and now, so had Finn. The journey ahead was uncertain, but one thing was clear: He would not let the darkness win. He was Finn, the curious fox, the chosen one, and he would not rest until Everleaf was safe once more.

Chapter 6

The First Test

The forest was alive with the sounds of dawn as Finn began his journey deeper into the heart of Everleaf. But beneath the chorus of birdsong and the rustle of leaves, there was an undercurrent of something darker, something that whispered of danger and uncertainty. The realization that he was the one chosen by the Great Willow had settled over him like a cloak—both a mantle of responsibility and a shield of purpose. But with that realization came the weight of what he must do and the knowledge that his first true test was now upon him.

The shadows cast by the rising sun stretched long and thin across the forest floor, and as Finn ventured farther from the safety of his familiar paths, he could feel the air growing cooler, the light dimmer, as if the very essence of

the forest was being sapped by an unseen force. The Great Willow's whispers, so clear the night before, had faded into the background, leaving Finn alone with his thoughts and the growing sense of foreboding that clung to him like a second skin.

He knew he was heading in the right direction—toward the part of the forest where the shadows had begun to take hold, where the life of the forest was ebbing away, leaving only darkness and decay in its wake. Finn's resolve was strong, but with every step, the doubts that had plagued him the night before began to creep back in, their voices insidious and persistent.

What if he wasn't strong enough? What if the darkness was too powerful, too cunning for him to outwit? The elders had believed in him, the Great Willow had chosen him, but what if they were wrong? What if he failed?

Finn shook his head, trying to dispel the thoughts that threatened to undermine his resolve. He couldn't afford to think that way, not now. The forest needed him to be strong, to be brave, to be the fox that the prophecy had spoken of. He took a deep breath, steadying himself, and pressed on, determined to see this through.

As he ventured deeper into the forest, the signs of the darkness grew more pronounced. The trees, once towering and majestic, now seemed twisted and gnarled, their branches reaching out like skeletal fingers. The ground beneath his paws was soft and damp, stained with the sickly brown of decaying leaves. The air was thick with the scent

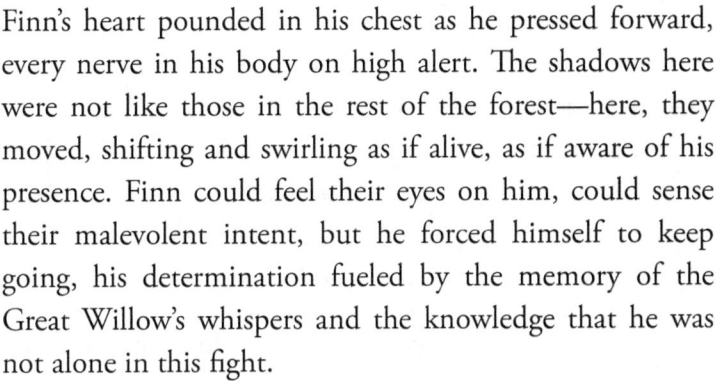

of rot, and the once vibrant colors of the forest had faded to muted grays and browns as if the life had been drained from the very soil.

Finn's heart pounded in his chest as he pressed forward, every nerve in his body on high alert. The shadows here were not like those in the rest of the forest—here, they moved, shifting and swirling as if alive, as if aware of his presence. Finn could feel their eyes on him, could sense their malevolent intent, but he forced himself to keep going, his determination fueled by the memory of the Great Willow's whispers and the knowledge that he was not alone in this fight.

It wasn't long before he reached a clearing—a place where the darkness had taken hold with a ferocity that sent a shiver down his spine. The trees here were little more than lifeless husks, their bark blackened and cracked, their branches hanging limp and devoid of leaves. The ground was bare, the grass was dead and brittle, and the air was thick with the stench of decay.

But it was the figure at the center of the clearing that made Finn's blood run cold. It was the same shadowy presence he had encountered before, but now it was more distinct, more solid as if it had fed on the darkness around it and grown stronger. The figure stood tall and menacing, its form shifting and writhing like smoke, its eyes—if they could be called that—glowing with an eerie, unnatural light.

Finn froze, his breath catching in his throat as he stared at the figure. It was watching him; he knew it, though he

couldn't see its face, couldn't make out any details beyond the shifting shadows that made up its form. The air around it was cold, the kind of cold that seeped into your bones, making your heart stutter and your breath falter.

For a moment, Finn was paralyzed by fear, his mind racing with the urge to turn and flee, to escape this place and the darkness that seemed to press in from all sides. But then, the whispers of the Great Willow came back to him, faint but clear, reminding him of his purpose, of the prophecy, of the trust that had been placed in him.

He couldn't run, not now. Not when the forest needed him.

Drawing on every ounce of courage he had, Finn took a step forward, his legs trembling beneath him but his resolve unyielding. The figure didn't move, didn't react, but Finn could feel its gaze on him, could sense the malice that radiated from it like a tangible force. It was as if the darkness itself had taken form and given life to the shadow that stood before him.

"What do you want?" Finn's voice was steady, though his heart was pounding in his chest. He wasn't sure if the figure could understand him, wasn't even sure if it was truly alive in the way he understood life, but he had to try. "Why are you doing this? Why are you destroying the forest?"

The figure remained silent, but the shadows around it seemed to pulse, to throb with a life of their own, as if in response to his words. Finn took another step forward, his fear now tempered by a growing anger, a righteous fury that burned in his chest like a fire.

"This is my home," Finn continued, his voice growing stronger. "These are my friends, my family. I won't let you destroy it. I won't let you win."

For a moment, the air was still, the silence heavy and oppressive. And then, the figure moved, its form shifting and elongating, the shadows around it swirling with an intensity that made Finn's fur stand on end. It was as if the darkness itself were responding to him, reacting to the defiance in his voice, the resolve in his heart.

The figure seemed to grow larger, more menacing, the cold around it deepening until it was almost unbearable. But Finn held his ground, his heart pounding, his breath coming in short, sharp bursts. He could feel the darkness pressing in on him . . . the weight of it on his chest, suffocating him, but he refused to back down.

And then, just as suddenly as it had begun, the figure stopped. The shadows around it stilled, the cold receded slightly, and for a fleeting moment, Finn thought he saw something in the darkness—something familiar, something that tugged at the edges of his memory.

But before he could make sense of it, the figure dissolved, melting back into the shadows and disappearing as if it had never been there at all. The clearing was empty now, the darkness that had suffused it beginning to lift though the signs of its presence remained—the dead trees, the withered grass, and the lingering scent of decay.

Finn stood there, his legs trembling, his heart still pounding in his chest. He had done it: He had faced the darkness,

confronted the shadowy figure, and survived. But as the adrenaline began to wear off, as the reality of what had just happened began to sink in, Finn felt a wave of exhaustion wash over him, and the weight of the encounter pressed down on him like a heavy blanket.

He had faced his first test, had confronted the darkness more directly than ever before, but he knew that this was only the beginning. The figure he had seen and the shadows that had overtaken the clearing were just a part of something larger, something far more dangerous. And though he had survived this encounter, Finn knew that the true battle was still ahead.

Taking a deep breath, Finn turned and began to make his way back through the forest, his steps slow and measured. The sun was rising higher now, the light growing stronger, but the shadows still lingered at the edges of his vision, a reminder of the darkness that was still out there, waiting.

As he walked, Finn's mind raced with questions, with doubts, but there was also a new resolve, a new strength that had been kindled by the encounter. He had faced his fear, had confronted the darkness, and though he had been shaken, he had not been defeated. The Great Willow's whispers echoed in his mind, reminding him of the prophecy, of the trust that had been placed in him.

Finn was ready for whatever came next. The darkness might be strong, but he was stronger. He would find the source of the shadows, would uncover the truth, and he would stop it, no matter the cost.

The First Test

The first test was over, but the journey had only just begun. Finn was determined to see it through, to protect his home, his forest, and all those who lived within it. The battle against the darkness was far from over, but Finn knew one thing for certain: He would not face it alone.

The forest was with him; the Great Willow's whispers were guiding him, and the resolve in his heart burned brighter than ever. Finn would not rest until the shadows were banished, until the light returned to Everleaf, until the prophecy was fulfilled.

Chapter 7

The Shadow Beneath the Leaves

The air in the forest felt different, heavier as Finn made his way through the trees, and the sunlight filtered through the canopy in narrow, hesitant beams. The shadows cast by the branches above seemed to stretch and twist unnaturally as if they were alive, shifting and undulating with a purpose of their own. The forest, once so familiar and comforting, had become a place of uncertainty, a landscape where every step forward felt like a descent into the unknown.

The encounter in the clearing had left Finn shaken, but more than that, it had left him with questions that gnawed at the edges of his mind, demanding answers that seemed just out of reach. The figure he had faced, the darkness that had gathered around it, was no ordinary shadow. It was something far more insidious, something that seemed

to feed on the very essence of the forest, draining it of life and light.

But what troubled Finn most was the feeling that the darkness was not just external. As he moved through the forest with the whispers of the Great Willow echoing faintly in his mind, he couldn't shake the sense that the shadow wasn't just something that lurked in the physical world. It was deeper, more pervasive as if it were a reflection of something within—something that had taken root in the hearts of the forest's inhabitants.

Finn's thoughts were interrupted by a sudden movement ahead. He froze, his ears pricking up, his senses on high alert. The forest had grown eerily quiet as the usual sounds of rustling leaves and chattering creatures were conspicuously absent. There was a tension in the air, a sense that something was watching him, waiting.

Cautiously, Finn moved forward, his paws silent on the forest floor. The path before him was narrow, lined with dense underbrush that seemed to close in around him as he walked. The shadows here were thicker, darker, and as he ventured deeper, the light from above grew dimmer, until it was little more than a faint, ghostly glow.

It wasn't long before Finn found himself in another clearing, though this one was different from the last. The trees that surrounded it were tall and twisted, their branches interwoven like a cage, blocking out most of the light. The ground was bare, the grass withered and brown, as if life had long since fled this place.

The Shadow Beneath the Leaves

In the center of the clearing stood the same shadowy figure he had encountered before, but this time it was more defined, its form sharper and more solid. It stood tall and still, its dark shape outlined against the pale, sickly light that filtered through the branches. The air around it was cold, colder than Finn had ever felt before, and as he approached, he could feel the temperature drop further, the chill sinking into his bones.

For a long moment, neither Finn nor the figure moved; the silence between them grew heavy and oppressive. Finn's heart pounded in his chest, but he forced himself to stand his ground, his eyes fixed on the shadow before him. There was something different about it this time—something that made his fur stand on end, which sent a shiver down his spine.

And then, without warning, the figure moved. It didn't walk or glide as before; instead, it seemed to shift and stretch, its form elongating and expanding until it covered the entire clearing in darkness. The shadows spread like ink, pooling at Finn's feet, climbing up the trunks of the trees, swallowing the light until there was nothing left but darkness.

Finn's breath caught in his throat as he realized what was happening. The darkness wasn't just around him; it was reaching for him, creeping up his legs, seeping into his fur, wrapping around him like a suffocating blanket. He could feel it pressing against his chest, squeezing the air from his lungs, pulling him down into its depths.

The Shadow Beneath the Leaves

Panic surged through him, and for a moment, Finn was overwhelmed by the urge to run, to escape the darkness that was closing in around him. But then the whispers of the Great Willow came back to him, faint but clear, cutting through the fear that threatened to consume him.

"Do not give in," the whispers seemed to say. "The darkness has no power over you unless you let it. Stand firm, young one. You are stronger than you know."

With a monumental effort, Finn forced himself to breathe, to focus on the whispers, on the strength that the Great Willow had instilled in him. He could feel the darkness pressing in, trying to crush him, to pull him down, but he refused to yield. He was Finn, the fox chosen by the prophecy, the one who would stand against the darkness. He would not be defeated.

As if sensing his resolve, the darkness hesitated, the pressure around him lessening slightly. Finn took the opportunity to push back, to assert his will against the shadow that sought to consume him. He could feel the cold seeping into his bones, could feel the weight of the darkness trying to drag him down, but he stood his ground, refusing to be swallowed by it.

And then, just as suddenly as it had begun, the darkness retreated. The shadows pulled back, releasing their grip on him, shrinking away until they once again formed the outline of the figure in the center of the clearing. The cold air began to warm slightly, and the suffocating pressure lifted, leaving Finn gasping for breath.

But the figure remained, its dark form still and silent, as if waiting for something. Finn, shaken but unbowed, took a step forward, his eyes narrowing as he studied the shadowy presence. There was something about it—something that tugged at the edges of his mind, which felt strangely familiar, as if he had seen it before, in some half-remembered dream.

Before he could make sense of the feeling, the figure spoke—not with words but with a voice that resonated deep within him, a voice that bypassed his ears and spoke directly to his heart.

"Fear . . . doubt . . . ," the voice whispered, cold and hollow. "These are the seeds from which I grow. You cannot escape them . . . cannot escape me. I am within you, as I am within all who dwell in this forest."

Finn's heart skipped a beat as the realization hit him. The darkness, the shadow—it wasn't just an external force. It was something deeper, something that had taken root within him, within the forest itself. It was a manifestation of the fear, doubt, and uncertainty that had been festering within them all, feeding on their anxieties, growing stronger with every passing day.

The figure's words echoed in his mind, the truth of them sinking in. The darkness wasn't just something that had come from outside; it was something that had been there all along, hidden beneath the surface, waiting for the right moment to emerge. And now, it was feeding on the fear and doubt that had spread through the forest like a disease.

The Shadow Beneath the Leaves

But even as the truth of the figure's words settled over him, Finn felt a surge of defiance rise within him. Yes, the darkness was within him, within the forest, but that didn't mean it couldn't be fought. Fear and doubt might be powerful, but they weren't invincible. They could be confronted and overcome.

With a deep breath, Finn took another step forward, his eyes locked on the shadowy figure. "You're right," he said, his voice steady despite the tremor in his chest. "You are fear; you are doubt. But you don't have to win. I can still fight you. We can still fight you."

The figure didn't respond, but the shadows around it seemed to pulse, to throb with a dark energy that made Finn's fur stand on end. He could feel the tension in the air, the weight of the darkness pressing down on him, but he refused to back down.

"This forest," Finn continued, his voice growing stronger, "is more than just a collection of trees and creatures. It's a place of hope, of life, of unity. The Great Willow's roots run deep, and they connect us all. You might have taken hold here, might have found a way to grow in the cracks, but you don't own this forest. We do."

For a moment, the darkness seemed to hesitate, as if unsure how to respond to Finn's words. And then, slowly, the shadows began to retreat, shrinking back toward the figure, the cold air warming slightly as the pressure lessened.

Finn watched as the figure dissolved once again, the shadows dispersing like smoke in the wind. The clearing,

though still dim and lifeless, felt less oppressive now, the weight of the darkness lifting, if only slightly.

He had done it—once again; he had faced the shadow, confronted the darkness within and without, survived. But as he stood there, catching his breath, Finn knew that this was only the beginning. The darkness was still out there, still lurking in the shadows, still feeding on the fears and doubts that lingered in the hearts of the forest's inhabitants.

But now, Finn understood what he was truly up against. The darkness wasn't just an enemy to be fought with tooth and claw—it was something that had to be confronted within, something that had to be understood, to be faced with courage and resolve.

With a newfound sense of determination, Finn turned and began to make his way back through the forest, his mind racing with the implications of what he had just experienced. The Great Willow's whispers echoed in his mind, guiding him, encouraging him, reminding him that he was not alone in this fight.

The battle against the darkness was far from over, but Finn was ready. He had faced the shadow beneath the leaves, had seen the darkness that lurked within, and he was more determined than ever to stop it. The forest was his home, and he would do whatever it took to protect it, to banish the darkness, to restore the light.

As he walked, the first rays of sunlight began to pierce the canopy above, casting the forest in a soft, golden glow. Finn lifted his head, his eyes bright with the light of a new day,

the light of a new understanding. Although the journey ahead was uncertain and the challenges great, Finn knew one thing for sure: He would not rest until the darkness was defeated, until the light returned to Everleaf, until the prophecy was fulfilled.

The shadow beneath the leaves had been revealed, but it had also been challenged. And now, it was time for Finn to finish what he had started. The battle had only just begun, but Finn was ready for whatever lay ahead. The forest was with him, the Great Willow's whispers were guiding him, and the resolve in his heart was burning brighter than ever.

Finn would not let the darkness win. He was the chosen one, the fox of the prophecy, and he would see this through to the end.

Chapter 8

A Glimpse of the Path Ahead

The morning sun crept slowly over the horizon, casting long, golden beams across the forest floor. Finn stood at the edge of the clearing where he had faced the shadow, his breath steady, his heart now resolved. The encounter had left him with a deep understanding of the battle ahead—a battle not just against an external force, but against the very fears and doubts that lurked within him and within the hearts of all who called Everleaf home. But as he gazed into the woods illumined by the dappled light filtering through the leaves above, he knew that this was only the beginning.

The air was fresh, carrying with it the scent of damp earth and the distant melody of birds beginning their day. Yet, there was a quiet urgency to the whispers of the Great Willow that reached Finn's ears, a subtle yet undeniable

push that urged him onward. He closed his eyes, allowing the whispers to fill his mind, to guide his thoughts. The tree's voice, ancient and wise, spoke not in words but in a language of feeling, of intuition, of understanding that transcended speech.

"Your journey is far from over," the whispers seemed to say, resonating deep within Finn's core. "What you have faced is but a shadow of the greater darkness that lies ahead. The path you must take is long and winding, filled with trials that will test your spirit, courage, and resolve. But you are not alone, young one. The forest is with you, and so too is the wisdom of the ages."

Finn opened his eyes, his gaze steady and clear. The Great Willow had always been a source of comfort, but now it was more than that; it was a guide, a mentor, a beacon that would light his way through the shadows that lay ahead. He felt the weight of the prophecy settle over him once more, but this time, it was not a burden. It was a responsibility, a purpose that filled him with a quiet strength.

The forest around him was still waking as the creatures of Everleaf emerged from their slumber to greet the new day. But Finn knew that beneath the surface, beneath the routine of daily life, there was a tension, a fear that the darkness had sown in the hearts of all who lived here. The shadow was not just a physical presence; it was a manifestation of their deepest fears and most deeply hidden doubts, and it was growing stronger with each passing day.

A Glimpse of the Path Ahead

The Great Willow's whispers guided Finn's thoughts, drawing his attention to the path that lay before him—a path not just through the physical forest, but through the very fabric of Everleaf's existence. The shadow had to be confronted, not just in its physical form but in the hearts and minds of the creatures who called this place home. And that would require more than courage; it would require wisdom, understanding, and a willingness to face the truths that lay hidden in the darkness.

As Finn pondered the journey ahead, the Great Willow's whispers shifted, becoming more focused, more direct. The tree was guiding him, showing him the way forward, revealing the steps he must take to uncover the truth about the shadow, to understand its origin, its purpose, and its ultimate goal.

"There is a path," the whispers seemed to say, "a path that winds through the deepest parts of the forest, through places where few have ventured, where the light is dim, and the shadows are thick. It is a path of trials, of riddles, of challenges that will test your very soul. But it is also a path of discovery, growth, and transformation. If you are to defeat the darkness, you must first understand it. And to understand it, you must walk this path, no matter where it may lead."

Finn felt a shiver of anticipation run through him, the thrill of the unknown mingling with the weight of the task ahead. He knew that the journey would not be easy, that it would take him to places he had never been, places where

the rules of the world he knew might not apply. But he also knew that this was what he had been chosen for, what the prophecy had foretold.

The path would take him deep into the heart of the forest, to places where the shadows were born, where the darkness had taken root. He would face riddles that challenged his mind, creatures that tested his courage, and truths that might shake the very foundation of his beliefs. But through it all, the Great Willow would be with him, its whispers guiding him, its wisdom lighting his way.

As the first rays of sunlight broke through the canopy, illuminating the clearing in a warm, golden glow, Finn took a deep breath, steeling himself for what lay ahead. The forest was alive with possibility, with the potential for both great danger and great discovery. He could feel the energy of the woods around him, the pulse of life that beat beneath the surface, and he knew that this was where he belonged—on this path, in this moment, ready to face whatever came next.

He turned to look back at the Great Willow, its massive form towering over the clearing, its branches swaying gently in the breeze. The whispers had quieted now, but the sense of purpose they had instilled in him remained strong. The path ahead was uncertain, but Finn was ready to walk it, ready to confront the darkness, to uncover the truth, and to fulfill the prophecy that had named him.

The Great Willow's final whispers echoed in his mind as he turned to face the forest, the path ahead stretching out before him like a ribbon of shadow and light.

A Glimpse of the Path Ahead

"Do not fear the darkness, young one," the whispers seemed to say. "For it is only in the darkness that the light can truly shine. Trust in yourself, in the strength of your heart, in the wisdom of the forest. The journey ahead is long, but you are ready. Go forth, and may the light guide your steps."

With those words echoing in his mind, Finn took his first step onto the path, his heart steady, his resolve unshakable. The forest closed in around him, the shadows deepening and the light dimming, but Finn walked forward with confidence, knowing that the Great Willow was with him, that the forest was with him, that he was not alone.

The path ahead was filled with uncertainty, with challenges that would test him in ways he could not yet imagine. But Finn was ready. He had faced the shadow and emerged stronger, more determined than ever to see this journey through to the end.

As he ventured deeper into the forest with the trees closing in around him and shadows growing thicker, Finn felt a sense of peace settle over him. The fear that had once gripped his heart had been replaced with a quiet confidence—a belief in himself, in the prophecy, and in the path that lay before him.

This was only the beginning of a much larger adventure, one that would take him to the farthest reaches of Everleaf, to places where the light barely touched, where the shadows held secrets long forgotten. But Finn was ready to face it all, ready to uncover the truth, to confront the darkness, and to bring light back to the forest he loved.

The Shadow Beneath the Leaves

The path ahead was daunting, but Finn knew that he was exactly where he needed to be. The journey had begun, and he would see it through, no matter the cost. With his heart full of resolve and his mind clear with purpose, Finn walked into the shadows, the light of a new day guiding his steps, the whispers of the Great Willow echoing in his soul.

The adventure had only just begun, but Finn knew one thing for certain: He would not stop until the light returned to Everleaf, until the darkness was banished, until the prophecy was fulfilled.

And so, with the forest at his back and the unknown before him, Finn continued on the path that would define his destiny. He was ready to face whatever challenges lay ahead, ready to uncover the secrets of the shadow, and ready to bring the light back to the heart of Everleaf.

Chapter 9

A Gathering Storm

The forest had always been a place of rhythm, a living symphony where each creature, each tree, and each breath of wind played its part in the grand design of Everleaf. But now, that symphony was being slowly, insidiously silenced. The harmony that had once defined the forest was unraveling, and with every passing day, the shadows grew longer, darker, and more malevolent.

Finn moved swiftly through the underbrush, his keen eyes scanning the surroundings for any signs of the creeping darkness that had begun to encroach upon more and more of the forest. The morning light was thin, pale, and hesitant as if it too feared the shadows that lay in wait beneath the canopy. There was a chill in the air, one that cut through Finn's fur and settled in his bones, a coldness that spoke

of more than just the change of season. It was the chill of something deeper, something far more dangerous.

As Finn ventured farther into the heart of Everleaf, he couldn't help but notice the changes that had taken hold. The trees, once proud and tall, now seemed to sag under an invisible weight, their leaves turning brittle and brown, their branches drooping as if in defeat. The vibrant green of the forest floor was marred by patches of withered grass; the once-clear streams were running slow and murky, their waters tinged with a sickly hue.

The signs were everywhere—subtle at first but growing more pronounced with each step Finn took. The shadow was spreading, its influence creeping into every corner of the forest, poisoning the very life force that sustained it. Finn's heart tightened as he realized just how vast the problem had become, how quickly the darkness was taking hold. It was no longer confined to the edges of Everleaf; it was moving inward, consuming more and more of the forest with each passing day.

The Great Willow's whispers, once a comforting presence, now carried a note of urgency, a warning that resonated deep within Finn's soul. He could feel the tree's concern and its awareness of the growing threat; the weight of that awareness pressed heavily upon him. The path ahead was becoming clearer, but so too was the magnitude of the task that lay before him.

Finn's mind raced as he pushed forward as the gravity of the situation settled over him like a shroud. He had faced

the shadow before, had confronted the darkness within and without, but this . . . this was different. The shadow was no longer a distant threat; it was here, now, spreading its tendrils of fear and doubt through the forest, weakening the resolve of all who lived within its bounds.

He could sense the change in the creatures he encountered along the way. Where once there had been greetings and camaraderie, now there was only silence, eyes cast downward, movements cautious and furtive. The birds that once filled the air with song were now quiet, their wings heavy as they flitted from branch to branch. The squirrels that once chattered happily in the treetops now moved in anxious, erratic patterns, their tails twitching with nervous energy.

As Finn made his way deeper into the forest, he came upon a familiar grove, a place that had once been a haven of peace and beauty. But now, the grove was a shadow of its former self. The flowers that had once bloomed in brilliant colors were wilted and brown, their petals scattered on the ground like ashes. The grass was dry and brittle underfoot, and the air was thick with the scent of decay.

At the center of the grove stood a massive oak, its trunk gnarled and twisted with age. Finn had always admired this tree and had often come here to rest beneath its wide, sheltering branches. But now, as he approached, he saw that the oak was in distress. Its leaves, once vibrant and full, were withered and falling, and the bark was peeling away in long, ragged strips. The tree seemed to groan under the weight of the shadow that had taken hold, its branches

sagging, its roots digging deep into the darkened earth as if searching for something that was no longer there.

Finn's heart ached at the sight, the full reality of the shadow's spread hitting him with brutal clarity. This was not just an attack on the forest—it was an attack on the very soul of Everleaf, on everything that had once made this place a sanctuary, a home. The shadow was not just a physical presence; it was a force that eroded hope, that fed on fear and doubt, that sought to break the spirit of the forest from within.

Finn closed his eyes and listened to the whispers of the Great Willow swirling around him, mingling with the sounds of the dying grove. He could feel the weight of the task before him, could sense the enormity of what he was being asked to do. The path ahead was clear, but it was also fraught with danger, with challenges that would test him in ways he had never imagined.

The creatures of Everleaf were losing hope. He had seen it in their eyes, felt it in the air that hung heavy with despair. The darkness was spreading faster than he had anticipated, and with it came a sense of inevitability, a fear that perhaps this was a battle they could not win.

But even as those thoughts swirled in his mind, Finn felt a spark of defiance ignite within him, a determination that refused to be extinguished. The Great Willow had chosen him, had entrusted him with the task of confronting this darkness, and Finn would not let that trust be in vain. He could not afford to lose hope, not when the forest needed him most.

A Gathering Storm

Finn took a deep breath, his resolve hardening. He had seen the shadow's effects, had felt its cold grip, but he also knew that it could be fought, that it could be resisted. The Great Willow's whispers spoke of a path, of challenges that would require all his courage and all his wisdom, but Finn was ready to face them.

He turned away from the dying grove, his steps deliberate and sure as he made his way back through the forest. The air was thick with tension, the sky above darkening with the promise of a storm, but Finn's mind was clear. The darkness was growing stronger, yes, but so too was his resolve. The storm was coming, but Finn would face it head-on, would do whatever it took to protect Everleaf and banish the shadow that threatened to consume it.

As he walked, the first drops of rain began to fall as the sky rumbled with distant thunder. The storm was gathering; darkness was pressing in from all sides, but Finn did not waver. He knew that this was just the beginning, that the challenges ahead would be greater than anything he had faced before, but he also knew that he was ready.

The creatures of Everleaf needed hope, needed someone to stand against the darkness, and Finn was determined to be that someone. The shadow might be growing stronger, but so too was his determination, his resolve to see this journey through to the end.

The storm was coming, but Finn would not be swept away by it. He would stand firm, would face the darkness with

everything he had, and he would not stop until the light returned to the forest, until Everleaf was safe once more.

With the rain falling around him and the thunder rumbling in the distance, Finn walked forward, his heart steady and his mind focused. The path ahead was uncertain, the challenges great, but he was ready. The battle against the shadow was far from over, but Finn knew one thing for certain: He would not rest until the storm had passed, until the light had returned, until the prophecy was fulfilled.

And so, with the storm gathering around him, Finn pressed on, his resolve unshakable, his heart full of determination. The darkness might be growing, but so too was his strength, his courage, his will to fight. The journey ahead was daunting, but Finn was ready to face it, ready to confront whatever challenges lay ahead, ready to bring light back to Everleaf.

Chapter 10

The Council's Decision

The storm that had been gathering over Everleaf finally broke as Finn made his way back to the heart of the forest, where the Great Willow stood sentinel over them all. The rain fell in heavy sheets, drumming against the leaves, cascading down the trunks of ancient trees, and turning the forest floor into a quagmire of mud and puddles. Thunder rolled through the sky, a deep, resonant sound that seemed to vibrate through the very bones of the earth. But even as the storm raged, there was a sense of purpose in the air, an urgency that could not be ignored.

Finn moved with determined strides, the cold rain soaking through his fur, but his heart was warm with resolve. The darkness was spreading, and time was running short. He

had seen the devastation firsthand, had felt the growing fear among the creatures of the forest. Now, more than ever, he needed guidance, needed to understand what must be done to confront the shadow that threatened to consume them all.

As he approached the clearing where the Great Willow stood, Finn saw that he was not alone. The elders of the forest had gathered beneath the ancient tree, their forms huddled together in solemn council. Willow the owl perched on a low branch, her feathers ruffled by the wind, her golden eyes sharp and watchful. Griselda the tortoise was there as well, her ancient shell gleaming with rainwater; her gaze was thoughtful and serious. Cormac the stag stood tall and proud, his antlers casting long shadows in the dim light, while Muriel the hare sat close to the ground, her ears twitching nervously with each crack of thunder.

These were the leaders of Everleaf, the ones who had guided the forest through countless seasons of change, through times of plenty and times of hardship. They had seen much and knew much, but even they could not hide the fear that flickered in their eyes, the uncertainty that weighed heavily on their hearts.

Finn approached the gathering with a mix of trepidation and determination. The Great Willow's whispers had led him here, had guided his steps through the storm, but now, standing before the council of elders, he felt the full weight of what was to come. The prophecy had named him, but the reality of that responsibility was only now beginning to sink in.

The Council's Decision

The elders turned to him as he stepped into the clearing, their eyes filled with a mixture of expectation and concern. Willow was the first to speak, her voice calm and measured, cutting through the sound of the rain like a knife through cloth.

"Finn," she said, her gaze steady and unwavering, "you have come at a critical time. The darkness is spreading faster than we anticipated, and the creatures of the forest are losing hope. We have called this council to determine our next steps, but we need your voice, your insight, to guide us."

Finn swallowed hard, feeling the eyes of the elders upon him. He had never imagined himself in this position— standing before the leaders of Everleaf, his opinions sought after, his decisions carrying weight. But the time for doubt was past. He had seen the shadow's effects, had felt its cold grip, and he knew that the forest could not survive much longer without decisive action.

"I've seen the shadow's work," Finn began, his voice steady despite the turmoil in his chest. "It's not just affecting the land; it's affecting the hearts of those who live here. The fear, the doubt . . . it's spreading, weakening us from within. We can't fight this darkness with strength alone. We need to understand it, to confront it on its own terms."

Griselda nodded slowly; her deep, resonant voice filled with the weight of ages. "You speak with wisdom, young Finn. The darkness is indeed more than a physical force; it is a reflection of the fears that have taken root in our

hearts, a manifestation of the doubts that have lingered in the shadows too long. To fight it, we must first confront the fears and doubts within ourselves."

"But how?" Muriel the hare asked, her voice trembling with anxiety. "How can we fight something that is a part of us, that feeds on our own weaknesses? The creatures of the forest are already losing hope. How can we possibly stand against such a force?"

Finn felt the eyes of the elders on him, waiting for his answer. He took a deep breath, drawing strength from the whispers of the Great Willow, which seemed to pulse through the very air around him, filling him with a sense of purpose, of clarity.

"We can't fight it alone," Finn said, his voice firm with conviction. "We must stand together, united by the strength of our bonds, by the trust we have in one another. The shadow feeds on fear, on isolation, on the cracks that form between us when we let doubt take hold. But if we confront those fears together, if we support each other, we can weaken the shadow's grip. We can push it back."

Cormac the stag stepped forward, his voice strong and clear. "Finn is right. We must not let the darkness divide us. The strength of Everleaf has always been in its unity, in the way we come together to protect what we love. This is a battle for the very soul of our home, and we must face it as one."

The elders murmured in agreement, their resolve hardening in the face of the growing threat. But Finn could see the

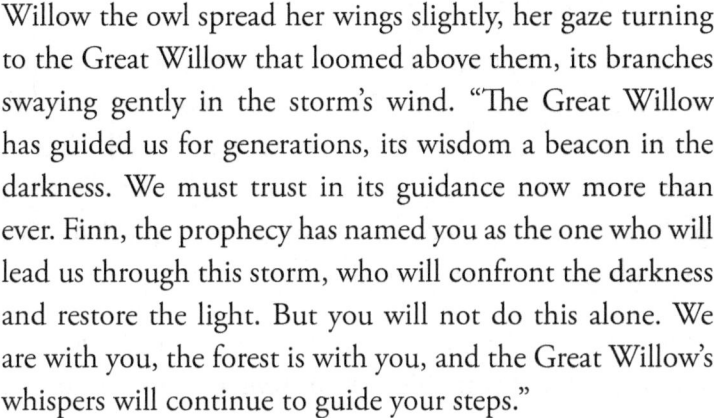

lingering doubt in their eyes, the fear that still clung to the edges of their hearts. This was not just a battle of strength; it was a battle of will and belief, and that made it all the more difficult.

Willow the owl spread her wings slightly, her gaze turning to the Great Willow that loomed above them, its branches swaying gently in the storm's wind. "The Great Willow has guided us for generations, its wisdom a beacon in the darkness. We must trust in its guidance now more than ever. Finn, the prophecy has named you as the one who will lead us through this storm, who will confront the darkness and restore the light. But you will not do this alone. We are with you, the forest is with you, and the Great Willow's whispers will continue to guide your steps."

Finn felt a surge of emotion swell within him—pride, fear, determination all mingling together in a powerful current. The council of elders was placing its trust in him, recognizing him as the key figure in the prophecy, as the one who would lead Everleaf through this time of darkness. But with that recognition came an immense responsibility, a weight that pressed down on his shoulders, heavy and unyielding.

Griselda, with the slow, deliberate movements of one who has seen many seasons, stepped forward and placed a gentle but firm paw on Finn's shoulder. "You are strong, Finn, stronger than you know. But even the strongest among us need guidance and wisdom. The Great Willow has shared its knowledge with us, and now we share it with you."

The Shadow Beneath the Leaves

With those words, Griselda reached into the folds of her ancient shell and produced a small, intricately carved stone—a token of Everleaf, a symbol of the forest's enduring strength. She handed it to Finn, her eyes filled with a quiet, unwavering confidence.

"This stone is a gift from the Great Willow," Griselda said, her voice low and solemn. "It holds a piece of the forest's spirit, a connection to the roots that bind us all. Keep it with you on your journey, and it will guide you when the path is unclear and remind you of the strength that flows through these woods, through you."

Finn accepted the stone with reverence, feeling the cool, smooth surface against his paw, the weight of it a comforting presence in his grip. It was more than just a token; it was a promise, a reminder that he was not alone in this fight, that the forest and its elders stood with him, no matter how dark the path ahead might become.

Cormac, his antlers gleaming with rainwater, stepped forward next, his gaze steady and filled with respect. "Take this as well," he said, offering a small, silver pendant shaped like a leaf. "It is a symbol of the forest's resilience, of the life that endures even in the face of darkness. Wear it as a reminder that no matter how strong the shadow may seem, the light of Everleaf will always find a way to shine through."

Finn accepted the pendant, feeling its cool weight around his neck as Cormac placed it over his head. The silver leaf gleamed in the dim light, a beacon of hope in the midst of

the storm, a symbol of the strength that would carry him through the challenges ahead.

The council of elders stood before him now, their eyes filled with a mixture of pride and expectation. Finn felt the gravity of the moment, the enormity of the task that lay before him, but he also felt something else—something deeper, something that resonated with the very core of his being.

It was a sense of purpose, of clarity, of knowing that this was what he had been chosen for, what he had been preparing for all his life. The prophecy had named him, had set him on this path, but it was his own heart, his own resolve that would see him through to the end.

Willow the owl, her voice soft and filled with ancient wisdom, spoke once more, her words carrying the weight of the ages. "The storm is upon us, Finn. The darkness is spreading, but so too is the light. You are the one who will lead us through this time of trial, who will confront the shadow and restore the balance to our home. Go forth with the blessing of the Great Willow, with the strength of Everleaf, and know that we are with you, every step of the way."

Finn nodded, his heart full, his resolve unshakable. The journey ahead was daunting, the challenges great, but he was ready. The council of elders had given him their blessing, their wisdom, their strength, and now it was up to him to fulfill the prophecy, to confront the darkness, to restore the light.

With the stone of Everleaf in his paw and the silver leaf pendant around his neck, Finn turned and faced the storm,

his heart steady, his mind clear. The battle against the shadow had only just begun, but Finn knew one thing for certain: he would not rest until the light had returned to the forest, until the prophecy was fulfilled.

And so, with the council's blessing and the Great Willow's whispers guiding him, Finn stepped forward into the storm, ready to face whatever challenges lay ahead, ready to confront the darkness, ready to bring light back to Everleaf. The light of Everleaf would shine once more, and Finn would lead the way.

Chapter 11

The First Steps of the Journey

The storm had passed, leaving the forest of Everleaf drenched in a shimmering mist that clung to the leaves and settled in the hollows of the trees. The air was thick with the scent of damp earth and pine, and the world felt quiet, subdued, as if the very breath of the forest had been held in anticipation of what was to come. Finn stood at the edge of the clearing, where the Great Willow loomed like a guardian over the forest, its ancient branches swaying gently in the aftermath of the tempest.

The council of elders had dispersed, each returning to their duties with a renewed sense of purpose, but Finn remained, his gaze fixed on the path that led away from the heart of the forest and into the unknown. The weight of the silver leaf pendant around his neck and the stone of Everleaf in

his paw were comforting reminders of the blessings and trust the elders had bestowed upon him, yet they were also symbols of the immense responsibility he now carried.

Finn knew that the time had come to leave the familiar paths of Everleaf, to venture beyond the borders of the forest he had always known, and to confront the darkness that threatened to consume everything he held dear. The journey ahead would take him to places he had never imagined, to the farthest reaches of the world, where the light barely touched, and the shadows ran deep. But it was a journey he knew he had to undertake, not just for the forest, but for himself—to understand the darkness, to face it, and ultimately, to dispel it.

The whispers of the Great Willow were a constant presence in his mind, a gentle murmur that guided his thoughts, his steps, his resolve. They spoke of a path, a journey that would test him in ways he could not yet comprehend, but they also spoke of a purpose, a destiny that was intertwined with the very soul of Everleaf. Finn took a deep breath filling his lungs with the cool morning air, and with a final glance at the Great Willow, he turned and began to walk.

The first steps were the hardest, the most daunting. The path before him was narrow and winding, flanked by tall, ancient trees whose roots twisted and intertwined beneath the earth. The familiar sounds of the forest—birds chirping, leaves rustling, the distant babble of a stream—began to fade as Finn ventured deeper, replaced by an eerie stillness that settled over the land like a shroud.

The First Steps of the Journey

But Finn did not falter. The whispers of the Great Willow urged him onward, filling him with a sense of purpose, of resolve. This was the path he had been chosen to walk; the journey he had been destined to undertake. Though the shadows pressed in from all sides and though the light seemed to grow dimmer with each step, Finn's heart was steady, his mind clear.

The forest around him began to change as he moved farther from the center of Everleaf. The trees grew taller, their trunks thicker and more gnarled, their branches twisting together to form a dense canopy that blocked out much of the sunlight. The underbrush was thicker here, the air cooler, and the silence more profound. It was as if he had entered a different world, a place where the rules of the forest he knew no longer applied.

Finn's senses were on high alert, every rustle of leaves, every snap of a twig drawing his attention. He could feel the presence of the darkness, could sense it lurking just beyond the edge of his vision, waiting, watching. But he did not let fear take hold. He had faced the shadow before, had confronted the darkness within, and he knew that the true test was still to come.

As he continued along the path, Finn encountered the first signs that he was no longer in the Everleaf he had always known. The trees, once familiar and comforting, now took on strange, twisted shapes, their bark rough and cracked, their roots exposed like skeletal fingers grasping at the earth. The ground beneath his paws became uneven, dotted with

sharp stones and tangled roots that threatened to trip him with every step.

But it was not just the landscape that had changed. Finn soon realized that he was not alone. Strange creatures, unlike any he had ever seen, began to appear in the shadows, their eyes gleaming with an otherworldly light. They were small, almost indistinguishable from the shadows themselves, but their presence was unmistakable—a reminder that he was venturing into a place where the familiar rules of Everleaf did not apply.

One of these creatures, a small, shadowy figure with glowing yellow eyes, stepped into his path, its gaze fixed on Finn. It did not speak, but the air around it seemed to hum with energy, a silent challenge that hung between them like a taut string.

Finn stopped, his heart racing, but he forced himself to remain calm. This was his first real test, a confrontation not just with the darkness but with the unknown. The whispers of the Great Willow echoed in his mind, reminding him of his purpose, of the strength that lay within him.

"Who are you?" Finn asked, his voice steady despite the fear that gnawed at the edges of his consciousness. "What do you want?"

The creature did not respond, but its eyes seemed to bore into Finn's soul, searching, probing. Finn felt a cold shiver run down his spine, but he did not back down. He held the creature's gaze, his resolve hardening with each passing moment.

The First Steps of the Journey

The silence stretched on; the tension was thick in the air. And then, just as suddenly as it had appeared, the creature stepped aside, melting back into the shadows, its yellow eyes the last thing to fade into the darkness. The path was clear once more. The creature had tested him, had measured his resolve, and he had passed the first of many trials that awaited him on this journey.

With renewed determination, Finn continued along the path, the landscape growing stranger and more foreboding with each step. The trees became more twisted, their branches forming intricate patterns that seemed to shift and change as he passed beneath them. The ground was uneven, littered with strange stones and creeping vines that seemed to reach out for him as he walked by.

But Finn did not falter. The whispers of the Great Willow were a constant presence, guiding him, comforting him, reminding him of the purpose that drove him forward. The darkness was growing stronger, the shadows deeper, but so too was his resolve. He had been chosen for this, had been prepared for this, and he would not stop until he had fulfilled the prophecy, until the light had returned to Everleaf.

As he ventured farther from the heart of the forest, Finn began to encounter other creatures, each stranger and more enigmatic than the last. Some were large, towering over him with eyes that glowed like embers in the darkness, while others were small, almost invisible in the shadows, their presence felt more than seen. Each encounter was a test, a challenge that pushed him to his limits, but with each victory, Finn grew stronger, more confident in his abilities.

The Shadow Beneath the Leaves

But it was not just physical strength that Finn needed on this journey. The challenges he faced were not just tests of his body but of his mind and spirit. The darkness he was fighting was not just an external force; it was a reflection of the fears and doubts that lay within him, within all the creatures of Everleaf. To defeat it, he would need to confront those fears, understand them, and find the strength to overcome them.

The path was long and winding, taking Finn to the farthest reaches of Everleaf where the light barely touched, and the shadows ran deep. But with each step, Finn felt a growing sense of purpose, a clarity that had eluded him before. The whispers of the Great Willow were guiding him, showing him the way forward, and with each challenge he faced, he drew closer to understanding the true nature of the darkness and his role in dispelling it.

As the day drew to a close, the sun dipping low in the sky and casting long shadows across the land, Finn found himself standing at the edge of a vast, dark forest—a place where the trees were so tall and dense that they blotted out the sky, where the shadows were thick and impenetrable, and where the air was filled with a sense of foreboding that made his fur stand on end.

This was the edge of Everleaf, the boundary between the world he had always known and the unknown that lay beyond. Finn knew that the true journey was only just beginning, that the challenges he had faced so far were but a prelude to the trials that awaited him in the darkness.

The First Steps of the Journey

But he was ready. The Great Willow's whispers had prepared him for this, had given him the strength and resolve he needed to face whatever lay ahead. The darkness might be growing stronger, the shadows deeper, but so too was Finn's determination to see this journey through to the end.

With a deep breath, Finn took his first step into the dark forest, the shadows closing in around him, the path ahead uncertain and full of danger. But his heart was steady, his mind clear. He was not just walking this path for himself—he was walking it for all of Everleaf, for the creatures who depended on him, for the light that must be restored.

The journey had begun in earnest, and Finn was ready to face whatever challenges lay ahead. The darkness would not win, not while he still had breath in his body, not while the whispers of the Great Willow still guided his steps. The light would return to Everleaf, and Finn would be the one to bring it back.

With the shadows closing in around him, Finn walked forward into the unknown, his heart full of resolve, his mind focused on the task ahead. The path was long, and the challenges were great, but he knew that he was exactly where he needed to be, doing exactly what he was meant to do.

And so, with the light of Everleaf in his heart, Finn continued the journey that would define his destiny, ready to face the darkness, ready to fulfill the prophecy, ready to bring light back to the heart of the forest. The adventure was only just beginning, but Finn knew one thing for certain: He would

not stop until the darkness was defeated, until the light had returned, until Everleaf was safe once more.

Chapter 12
The Whispering Winds

The night had fallen softly over the forest, a velvet hush descending with the kind of reverence reserved for sacred spaces. Above, the sky stretched wide and watchful, adorned with glimmering constellations that blinked like the ancient eyes of time itself. The moon, low and solemn, bathed the treetops in silver, lending the woods a haunting kind of grace. Finn stood at the edge of a quiet glade, the whispers of the Great Willow pulsing in the back of his mind—a low, rhythmic beat like a distant drum guiding a weary traveler home.

The air was cool and fragrant with pine and moss, its stillness alive with unspoken memory. Finn drew a breath and exhaled slowly, feeling not emptiness, but a profound

wholeness rise within him. It was not peace born of resolution, but one forged in understanding—hard-earned, weathered, and deeply rooted in the knowledge that the journey, though far from over, had already changed him.

He recalled the beginning—when the call first stirred, faint as a dream, within the rustle of the Great Willow's leaves. Then, he had been uncertain, a young fox burdened with questions he didn't yet know how to ask. He had stood at the threshold of purpose, not yet ready to step through. But time and trial had done their work. Slowly, chapter by chapter, he had been carved into something more resilient, more aware, more awake.

The forest, too, had evolved. Where once there was harmony, now the shadow had deepened its hold. Its tendrils had crept farther, cloaking Everleaf in uncertainty. But in the midst of rising fear, Finn had chosen a different path. He had seen despair and refused to mirror it. He had glimpsed the dark and chosen, again and again, to walk toward the light.

And now, here—on the cusp between what had been and what was still to come—he felt the forest breathe with him. The Great Willow's whispers grew stronger, not in volume, but in clarity. They no longer felt like an external guide but an inner resonance—a rhythm that pulsed in his chest, a knowing that transcended words.

"You have come far, young one," the voice murmured within him, soft as a lullaby and steady as stone. "The road

ahead is veiled, but not void. Trust the light within you—it is stronger than the dark that surrounds."

Finn closed his eyes, not to shut the world out, but to hear more deeply. The doubts that once loomed like towering shadows had shrunk to quiet echoes. In their place stood something truer—a wisdom that didn't proclaim itself loudly, but revealed itself in calm, in courage, in presence.

When he opened his eyes, the horizon was beginning to shift. A faint blush of dawn gathered in the east, brushing the treetops with gold. And in that delicate interplay of night and day, of end and beginning, Finn saw it clearly: this was not closure. This was becoming.

The journey had not simply tested him—it had revealed him. Through fear and fire, through silence and solitude, he had discovered something essential. Not a power from without, but a truth from within: that the light he sought was already his to carry.

The wind stirred once more, lifting the leaves in a solemn chorus, the voice of the Great Willow weaving through the branches. "You are not the same as when you began. And you are not yet who you must become. But you are ready."

Finn bowed his head—not in defeat, but in reverence. Every step, every loss, every glimmer of hope had brought him to this threshold. And with the forest around him, the Great Willow behind him, and the rising dawn before him, he stepped forward.

The Shadow Beneath the Leaves

This was not the end. Nor was it merely the beginning of the next trial. It was the awakening of something greater.

And though the darkness still lingered, Finn now carried within him the unshakeable light of Everleaf.

The Forest Holds its Breath

Evening had fallen in Everleaf, but it was no ordinary dusk. The sky, veiled in a soft lilac hue, bled into the canopy above as if the trees themselves had exhaled their final breath of light. In the hush that followed, the world did not sleep. It listened.

Finn stood near the stream, not to hear the water—he had learned its song—but to feel the silence that surrounded it. There was no rush now. No urgent need to press forward, nor any voice—internal or otherwise—demanding his ascent. Only the stillness. Only the forest. Only himself.

The journey through shadow had changed him. The trials, the teachings, the whispers—each had carved something into his soul, not unlike the etchings the old tortoise bore

The Shadow Beneath the Leaves

Evening had fallen in Everleaf, but it was no ordinary dusk. The sky, veiled in a soft lilac hue, bled into the canopy above as if the trees themselves had exhaled their final breath of light. In the hush that followed, the world did not sleep. It listened.

Finn stood near the stream, not to hear the water—he had learned its song—but to feel the silence that surrounded it. There was no rush now. No urgent need to press forward, nor any voice—internal or otherwise—demanding his ascent. Only the stillness. Only the forest. Only himself.

The journey through shadow had changed him. The trials, the teachings, the whispers—each had carved something into his soul, not unlike the etchings the old tortoise bore on his shell. They were not wounds, but wisdom. Not burdens, but beginnings.

He thought of the crow, of knowledge and its many masks. Of the silent stream and the peace it required to truly hear. Of the tortoise, slow and deliberate, and the hidden strength that resided in patience.

Everleaf had not diminished. It had deepened. And so had he.

No, the forest was not a place to leave. It was a place to return to—again and again—until its lessons no longer whispered but roared with understanding. There were parts yet unexplored, within both the forest and himself. And he knew: the path ahead would not be outward, but inward. Into the roots. Into time. Into the truths that waited beneath the surface of stillness.

The Forest Holds its Breath

The air shifted. A soft rustle stirred the leaves—not from wind, but from something older. Something watching. Something waiting.

Finn turned toward the heart of Everleaf, and for the first time, he did not wonder what lay beyond.

He wondered what lay **within.**

The Whisper That Endures

The wind had shifted. Finn could feel it, though he could not yet name it. The air, once thick with the fragrance of damp earth and the quiet hum of leaves brushing against each other, now carried something weightier—something ancient, something waiting. The Shadow Beneath the Leaves had lifted, but in its absence, a new hush had settled upon Everleaf, as though the forest itself was holding its breath.

Finn stood beneath the Great Willow, his fur ruffled by the night's cool embrace. His mind swirled with the echoes of everything he had seen, everything he had learned. The battle of truth and deception had left its mark—not just upon Everleaf, but upon him. Yet, despite his newfound understanding, a question lingered, threading its way

through his thoughts like the whispered rustling of the trees: What now?

From deep within the roots of the Great Willow, something stirred. A sound, not unlike a sigh, reverberated through the ground, making the very soil tremble beneath Finn's paws. He lowered himself, ears pressed forward, alert. The whispers were back. Not the deceptive murmurs of the shadowed ones, but something different—gentler, wiser. A whisper not from darkness, but from time itself.

A single golden leaf, impossibly luminous under the moonlight, detached itself from the ancient branches above and floated downward, its descent measured, deliberate. Finn reached out a paw, allowing it to land softly against his fur. The moment it touched him, a warmth surged through his body— familiar, yet unknown.

And then, a voice.

Not loud, not forceful, but profound. A voice that had seen the rise and fall of forests, the changing of the stars, the shaping of wisdom over centuries. A voice that carried the weight of patience, the knowing of things that could not be rushed.

"The truth you seek will not be found in haste."

Finn's breath hitched. He knew, instinctively, that this voice did not belong to the Great Willow. No, this was something else. Something older. Something watching. The golden leaf pulsed softly, as if in agreement.

The Whisper That Endures

A faint ripple moved through the trees beyond him. A slow, deliberate sound—movement, but not of the wind. The leaves parted, revealing the curve of an immense shell glinting under the pale light.

A tortoise.

Griselda.

She moved with an unshaken grace, each step pressing an imprint upon the earth that would remain long after she had gone. Her eyes, vast pools of amber wisdom, held Finn's gaze as though she could see past his present and into all the paths yet to be walked.

"You hear them now, don't you?" she asked, her voice a low rumble, ancient as the stars above.

Finn swallowed. "The whispers? Yes. But they're different."

Griselda inclined her head. "Because they are not calling you to battle. They are calling you to understanding."

Finn's tail twitched, uncertainty pressing against the edges of his mind. "What am I supposed to do now?"

The tortoise regarded him for a long moment before answering. "You listen. You learn. You wait."

Finn's fur bristled. "Wait? But there's so much to—"

Griselda raised a clawed foot, silencing him with nothing more than a shift in her presence. "Knowledge without patience is like wind without form. You may chase it, but you will never grasp it. You will run, but you will never arrive."

The Shadow Beneath the Leaves

Finn fell silent.

The Great Willow let out another whisper, this time softer, as if to confirm what had been said. Finn's paws clenched against the earth. The battles he had fought had taught him the price of deception, the weight of truth. But patience? That was something he had never stopped to consider.

Griselda's eyes softened, and she stepped closer, placing her heavy foot deliberately in front of the other. "You wish to know the path ahead?"

Finn nodded.

She gestured toward the forest beyond. "Then you must walk it. Not as a warrior. Not as a seeker. But as a student of time itself."

The leaf against Finn's fur pulsed again. The whispers in the wind quieted, as though satisfied with his understanding.

Finn took a breath. A new journey was beginning, not with a battle, but with a lesson. One that would demand more of him than any fight ever had.

The truth was not merely something to be uncovered.

It was something to be earned.

And so, as the stars continued their slow waltz across the sky, Finn stepped forward—toward the unknown, toward the waiting wisdom of time.

Toward *The Tortoise's Timeless Wisdom.*

To Be Continued . . . .

Enjoy this exclusive sneak peek from the next
installment of Whispers of the Willow

THE
TORTOISE'S
Timeliness
WISDOM

✴ ·········· Book Two ·········· ✴

Whispers of the Willow:
The Chronicles of Finn and the Hidden Truth

The Slow Path Forward

The sun had just begun its ascent, casting long shadows across the forest floor, where the dew still clung to the leaves like tiny jewels. Finn stood at the edge of a path that was barely discernible beneath the dense undergrowth. It was as though the forest itself had forgotten this place, allowing time to weave its threads, undisturbed and unnoticed, into the fabric of the earth. The air was thick, almost heavy, with a stillness that pressed down on him, urging him to proceed with caution. Every instinct within him whispered that this was not a place to be rushed—that here, in this forgotten corner of Everleaf, haste would be met with resistance.

Finn took a deep breath, filling his lungs with the scent of damp earth and decaying leaves. The forest around him

seemed to hum with an ancient energy, a rhythm that was slow and deliberate, far removed from the urgency he had felt during the earlier parts of his journey. The path ahead was narrow, winding through trees that towered above him, their branches intertwined to form a canopy so thick that it allowed only the faintest traces of light to filter through. It was as if time itself had slowed here, each moment stretching out like a long shadow, leaving Finn with the unsettling sensation that he was moving through a world apart from the one he had known.

The first few steps were tentative, almost hesitant, as Finn tried to adjust to the unfamiliar pace. The ground beneath his paws was uneven, littered with fallen branches and the tangled roots of ancient trees that seemed to reach up from the earth like the gnarled fingers of some unseen giant. Every movement required careful consideration, every step a deliberate act of will. The urgency that had once driven him so fiercely now felt out of place as if it would disturb the delicate balance of this hidden part of the forest.

As he ventured deeper, the path grew narrower, the underbrush thicker, until it was no longer clear where the trail ended, and the forest began. Finn's progress slowed to a crawl, his sharp eyes scanning the ground ahead for any sign of the way forward. But the forest offered no clear direction, no obvious markers to guide him. Instead, it seemed to whisper a silent challenge: To move forward, Finn would need to slow down to match the rhythm of this place and become a part of the forest rather than an intruder upon it.

The Slow Path Forward

The discomfort was immediate and acute. Finn had always been quick, agile, his movements driven by a keen mind that thrived on action and discovery. But here, in this dense, slow-moving part of Everleaf, those qualities seemed more hindrance than help. His natural urge to push forward to find the next clue, the next challenge, was met with resistance at every turn. The forest seemed to resist his every move, forcing him to slow down, to take stock, to truly see what was around him.

And what he saw were the subtle signs of a presence far older and wiser than his own. The first of these signs was a worn path, almost invisible beneath the thick carpet of leaves, yet unmistakably there, a faint trail that wound its way through the trees like a thread through a tapestry. It was a path that had been walked many times, not by the hurried feet of those who sought to conquer the forest but by the slow, deliberate steps of one who understood its secrets.

Finn's heart quickened as he realized what this meant. These were Griselda's paths, the trails left behind by the wise tortoise who had moved through this forest with a patience and understanding that Finn could only aspire to. The realization was both comforting and humbling, a reminder that he was not alone in this journey, that others had walked this path before him, leaving behind the faintest traces of their wisdom for those who were willing to see.

He followed the path carefully, each step a conscious decision, each movement slow and deliberate. The farther he went, the more signs he found: ancient markings carved

into the trunks of trees, small piles of stones that had been carefully arranged, the faintest trace of a scent that was familiar and comforting. These were Griselda's markers, the signs of her presence, her wisdom, her understanding of the forest. They were there to guide him but only if he was willing to slow down, to see them, to truly appreciate the knowledge they held.

But slowing down was not easy. Finn could feel impatience bubbling just beneath the surface, a restless energy that urged him to move faster, to push forward, to find the answers he sought. It was an urge that had served him well in the past and had driven him to confront the darkness that threatened Everleaf. But here, in this part of the forest, that same urgency felt out of place, almost dangerous. It was as if the forest itself was testing him, challenging him to let go of his need for speed and action and to embrace a different way of moving through the world.

The struggle was internal as much as it was external. Finn could feel the tension in his muscles, the impatience in his thoughts, the frustration that came from moving so slowly when every instinct screamed at him to go faster. But he knew, deep down, that this was a lesson he needed to learn, that the forest was offering him something far more valuable than speed or strength. It was offering him wisdom, the kind of wisdom that could only be gained through patience; stillness; and the deliberate, careful observation of the world around him.

As the day wore on, Finn began to notice changes in himself. The tension in his body slowly began to ease, the restlessness in his mind giving way to a quiet, almost meditative state. The path ahead was no longer a challenge to be overcome but a journey to be experienced. Each step was a moment of connection with the forest—each movement an opportunity to learn, to grow, to understand.

And with that understanding came a deeper appreciation for the world around him. The forest was no longer just a place to be explored; it was a living, breathing entity with its own rhythms, its own pace, its own wisdom. The trees, the earth, the very air seemed to pulse with a slow, deliberate energy that Finn could feel in his bones, a rhythm that he was beginning to match with his own movements and thoughts.

The discomfort that had plagued him at the beginning of his journey was fading, replaced by a sense of peace and connection. Finn could feel the presence of Griselda all around him, guiding him, teaching him through the subtle signs she had left behind. It was a presence that was both comforting and challenging, a reminder that he still had much to learn, but also that he was on the right path.

As the sun began to set, casting long shadows across the forest floor, Finn came to a small clearing. The air was warm, filled with the scent of wildflowers and the soft hum of insects. It was a peaceful place that invited stillness and reflection. And as Finn stood there, feeling the last rays of the sun on his fur, he realized that he had begun to learn the lesson the forest had been trying to teach him all along.

The Shadow Beneath the Leaves

The slow path forward was not a burden, not a challenge to be overcome but a gift. It was an opportunity to see the world in a new way, to understand the deep, ancient wisdom that time and patience could offer. It was a lesson that Finn knew he would carry with him, a lesson that would shape his journey in ways he could not yet fully understand.

And as the first stars began to appear in the sky, Finn lay down in the soft grass, his heart filled with quiet, peaceful contentment. The path ahead was still long, the challenges still great, but he was ready to move forward, slowly, deliberately, with the wisdom of the forest as his guide.

Anthony Ofili Nwosisi is a scholar, storyteller, and architect of insight who writes at the edge where artificial intelligence confronts human complexity. As a doctoral researcher in Explainable AI (XAI) at the University of Amsterdam, he explores how intelligent systems reshape creativity, redefine failure, and alter the pathways of organizational learning and innovation. His academic work probes not only how machines process data—but how humans adapt, err, and evolve when those machines become decision-makers. His focus is clarity in complexity. Truth amidst opacity.

But Anthony's voice does not stop at research. It resounds through narrative.

He is the visionary behind *Whispers of the Willow: The Chronicles of Finn and the Hidden Truth*—a profound twelve-book saga that weaves timeless virtues into the pulse of an enchanted, yet deeply human world. These are not children's books, nor are they merely fantastical tales. They are carefully layered odysseys that teach resilience, awaken moral courage, and guide the reader—young or old—through the hidden architecture of wisdom.

Whether decoding the neural scaffolding of AI systems or constructing allegorical universes where characters face the agony of choice and the burden of knowledge, Anthony's work is unified by one pursuit: ***to awaken discernment in an age numbed by automation.***

He does not separate science from story, nor mind from soul. He writes to reconcile them.

To pierce the fog. To restore memory. To illuminate truth.

www.ingramcontent.com/pod-product-compliance
Lightning Source LLC
Chambersburg PA
CBHW072356020726
47506CB00004B/1149